THE EGO PLAYS

James Ley

THE EGO PLAYS

Spain

I Heart Maths

Up

OBERON BOOKS
LONDON

WWW.OBERONBOOKS.COM

First published in 2011 by Oberon Books Ltd
521 Caledonian Road, London N7 9RH
Tel: +44 (0) 20 7607 3637 / Fax: +44 (0) 20 7607 3629
e-mail: info@oberonbooks.com
www.oberonbooks.com

A catalogue record for this book is available from the British
Library.

ISBN: 978-1-84943-230-6

Cover photgraphy of Matthew McVarish
in *I Heart Maths* by Leslie Black

Printed and bound by CPI Group (UK) Ltd, Croydon, CR0 4YY.

Contents

Introduction

I didn't plan to write a gay play but then I wrote three. Although I am not sure if gayness is the main thing these plays have in common. In fact the main thing that unites these plays is self-indulgence, and at the heart of each play is a gay man asking a lot of questions… about himself.

These questions range from scientific and philosophical musings to angst-ridden pleas for enlightenment. They come from men who have become so trapped in their own situations that they can no longer successfully connect with the outside world.

Up is a play about despair, *I Heart Maths* is a play about love and *Spain* is a play about moving on. Together they present the cognitive processes of three men who have allowed personal problems to grow to monstrous proportions.

Michael, the main character in *I Heart Maths*, who having failed to discover a genetic model for homosexuality generating testable predictions, is ultimately redeemed by love. Ally, the protagonist in *Spain*, has been less lucky in love. He replays and relives his past in minute detail as he searches his checkered sexual history for an escape from mental torment and heartache. The most unfortunate of the three protagonists is Robert in *Up*, a young gay teacher, confined to a psychiatric hospital following a breakdown. Urban myths, intrusive thoughts and obsessive compulsive disorder have created a terrifying world, which worsens the more he probes and pulls it apart.

In each of these plays excessive self-analysis leads to the main characters taking desperate measures, though frequently also leading to humorous consequences. But while these plays are comedies, exploring the perils of taking oneself too seriously, they are not intended to be cruel. Instead they set their characters free by making their worst fears come true and then taking them somewhere new.

James Ley

SPAIN

Spain was first performed on Tuesday, 25 October 2011 for Glasgay! Festival at the Citizens Theatre, Glasgow.

Co-created and performed by Mark Kydd

CREW

Director, Rosalind Sydney

Production Manager,
Stage Manager and Lighting Designer, Neil B. Anderson

Designer, Kate Temple

Video Designer, Jonathan Ley

Sound Designer, Danny Krass

Production Assistant, Katie McNutt

Producer, Steven Thomson

1.

Lights up on a terrified ALLY in Ricky's Cabaret Bar. He's wearing a diagonally striped blue and white dress and a long dark wig, tied back by a thin metallic headband. He's in the throes of performing a tribute to Remedios Amaya's 1983 Eurovision performance of ¿Quién maneja mi barca?

At a certain point in the performance he becomes aware of the audience. The more he looks at individual faces, the more he loses confidence in his act. His eyes rest on a particular gentleman and he freezes. ALLY stares at him for a few beats and then leaves the stage.

2.

It's early evening in ALLY's apartment, which is empty except for a partially packed suitcase with a laptop balanced on top of it. There is a box on the floor by the suitcase stuffed with photographs, tickets, flyers and postcards. On the walls of the apartment there's a scattered mosaic of photographs and spaces where photographs used to be.

ALLY enters. He's in office-wear, but looks dishevelled. He's carrying a bottle of wine and an unopened card. He puts down the wine and opens the card. On the front it says 'HASTA LA VISTA'. Since there's nowhere else to stand the card he stands it on the floor by the suitcase. He sits on the floor, opens the wine and pours himself a glass.

ALLY: *(Holding the glass up.)* Hasta la vista.

He drinks. He opens the laptop and a Gaydar alert sounds. He types furiously. A message pings in response. He types again. Another message pings. He types again and then puts the laptop down. During the next speech he takes a selection of flyers and postcards from the box and lays them out on the floor in front of him.

It's *(insert today's date)* and I have just arranged to meet Canarian Boy 85 WE – well endowed. Which probably means – *(ALLY makes a gesture with his pinkie.)* He'll be here in an hour, which gives me just enough time to…

ALLY stands up and looks at his suitcase and the remaining things he needs to pack. Distracted by one of the photos on the wall he goes over to it. It's a photo of a young woman in a gilt frame. The photo is illuminated.

ALLY: I'm leaving, Delores. I mean it this time.

The light on the picture fades. ALLY sits beside the suitcase. He picks up a postcard. It has a tacky image of naked women on the front. He reads –

I must be the first fucking Spanish to buy a postcard like this. I don't have any piece of paper when I come here today and you are not here so I buy her. Look at the tits. It's a shame you are not here. Hope you are OK. J. *(Turning over the postcard)* Look at the tits indeed? We all know how much you love tits. J.

ALLY rips the postcard up and puts the pieces on the floor. His attention is drawn to a tattered black and white flyer. He holds it up.

The Cabeza de Toro, Tenerife. *(Beat.)* Of course it's not really the Cabeza de Toro, it's really just the Bull's Head. Douglas – an ex-friend of mine – and I have Spanishified the name as it's the most English place in the world. How hilarious are we?

He holds up the flyer by a corner.

This is where it all began. It's 1990. I'm 21. Don't do the maths – all you need to know is that I'm older than I look. I look after myself. I always wear sunscreen and I haven't had any children.

ALLY jumps up.

PEDRO: You lookin' for a gay place? It's the Bull's 'ead.

ALLY: This is skinny Pedro the club rep and believe it or not, despite his camp English accent, he's actually from Spain. This is the second flyer skinny Pedro's given me. The first was for a live sex show.

PEDRO: Life Porno. Life Porno, you like? You looking for sexy girl, it's Life Porno.

ALLY: It's not really how I roll, Pedro. *(Reading the flyer.)* The Bull's Head Cellar Bar. British owned, British beer, pool and darts and bar snacks. *(Beat.) This* is a gay place?

PEDRO: That's what I said, innit? You looking for a gay place it's the Bull's Head.

ALLY: You're fucking right we're looking for a gay place, skinny Pedro. That's why Douglas and I came to Tenerife. The Bull's Head is a fucking dump and it couldn't be any less Spanish if Angie Watts was stood behind the bar. And the only gay-looking thing I can see in there is Douglas. It's looking like skinny Pedro's given us a bum steer until I notice the barman, with his Tom Selleck moustache, looking over at us.

TERRY: You looking for a gay place?

ALLY: Douglas and I say nothing.

TERRY: You'll have to come back later.

ALLY: Terry winks at me and shrieks with laughter. Next to him, the blousy barmaid with the perm laughs too. This is Trish.

TERRY: I don't know what you're laughing at, Trish, no one said they were going to shag you.

ALLY: Terry laughs loudly, trying to cover up the fact that his cruel remark made little or no sense.

ALLY: Douglas and I leave but heed Terry's advice and return later. Not later enough though, as when we come back the Cabeza de Toro is empty and we're treated to an hour or so of Terry's chat – ever dropping a barbed bon mot, arching an eyebrow and ripping into Trish.

TERRY: Either one of you boys has farted, or Tricia is stood behind me, breathing down my neck.

ALLY: This makes Trish laugh – she is of course stood behind him. Terry pretends to be startled.

13

TERRY: Who needs a mirror ball? Trish laughs and the whole room is lit up with silver amalgam!

ALLY: Trish scurries off to collect some glasses while Terry pretends to warm his hands in front of Douglas' sunburnt face. Douglas was spread-eagled on the beach all afternoon under a thin application of factor fuck all. But then he was forever doing things without protection. Douglas and I went to school together in Edinburgh. He was in the year below me, but he became gay first and left school before I did, taking to the skies as a trolley dolly for Air 2000 – or Legs in the Air 2000 as we called it. He got us cheap flights to Tenerife – which is how come we're here. *(Beat.)* Terry flicks through the TV channels settles on one and turns to us.

TERRY: Have you boys met Crystal? No? Well it's my very great pleasure to introduce you to her. Everyone on the island watches this shit. Crystal and her mother were separated early in life – can't remember why, it's not important. Let's say the mother was a junkie. However, their paths cross again and tragedy ensues – *(Pointing at the screen.)* now you see that stripper? She used to be a nun and she's pregnant with the butcher's baby, but she doesn't know that the butcher is her second cousin…

ALLY is distracted by one of the postcards on the floor. He grabs it and reads.

I know I said the last time that it was the last time. Can we have one more last time? J.

ALLY rips up the postcard and puts the pieces with the others.

ALLY: I tear myself away from Crystal and get up to go to the loo and there are two cute guys playing pool. Terry notices me staring at them.

TERRY: Oh yeah? *(Beat.)* The big one – that's Roberto – he's deaf-mute – sometimes I wish I was that way inclined, like when I'm doing a double shift with Tricia.

ALLY: Tricia cackles with laughter.

TERRY: Shriek like that one more time, Patricia, and I'll glass your face, sweetheart. *(Beat.)* The little one is Jesús and everyone wants to fuck him. He doesn't speak a word of English so you'll have to use the universal language of gay – mince past him and don't forget to stick your arse out.

ALLY: I don't remember what happens next. I don't think I mince past him and I certainly don't stick my arse out. Cut to me walking back over to Douglas, flanked by Roberto and Jesús.

TERRY: Thought you'd take the pair of them, did you, you greedy bitch?

ALLY: 'Roberto is just driving us,' I say.

TERRY: So you've hit the jackpot then? *(Leaning in, whispering loudly.)* I've heard Jesús is big. He'll make your eyes water.

ALLY: I arrange to meet Douglas on the beach the next morning and leave. Jesús lives with his mother – he's only eighteen after all – so I'm taken to Roberto's place, as he lives alone. In return for his hospitality we are forced to look through his photograph collection. For the first couple of albums I provide an enthusiastic say-what-you-see commentary – 'That must be your brother. You're a very tall family aren't you? Quite unusual for Spain. Ooh look at Mum, she's eating again…' Forty-five minutes later and I'm scowling and turning over the pages without even looking at them. 'Does your grandmother ever wash that fucking blouse, the dirty bitch?' I'm dying to say.

Jesús and I finally make it to the bedroom and I lie with my head on his chest as he sings softly to me a song about a donkey – something from his childhood, sweet and melodic, not Una Paloma Blanca –

ALLY takes out a small pendant chain in the shape of Italy. He holds it up.

He gave me this pendant. It's a map of Italy.

DOUGLAS: What did he give you that for? Doesn't he know what shape his own country is?

ALLY: Douglas said, the next day.

DOUGLAS: I bet he has a whole drawer full of pendants that he dishes out to anyone who gives him a fuck.

ALLY: Who cares what Douglas thinks?

ALLY puts the pendant around his neck.

The gift of the pendant makes me feel special, even though it acts like a rite of back passage to Jesús. Terry was right, Jesús has a lot going for him. *(Beat.)* I wake the next morning, Roberto's in the shower and Jesús is desperate to pee so he bangs repeatedly on the bathroom door, hoping the deaf guy stood under running water will respond, but strangely he doesn't. Jesús comes into the bedroom, picks up an empty beer bottle and pisses into it. I'm horrified – not just because I can't believe I managed to fit that thing inside me – but I'm also in awe – he's so unapologetic, so skilful – it's an act of unflustered, liberated Spanishness. *(Pause.)* And then there's a racket outside and banging on Roberto's door. It's Jesús' mother, she's on the war-path. I hide in the wardrobe and this feels like a scene from one of the Almodóvar films I've seen – bought on VHS from West and Wilde on Edinburgh's Dundas Street – *Women on the Verge* or *Pepi, Luci, Bom*. And it feels like I'm in the wardrobe forever, peering through the slatted door but Jesús' mother goes eventually and I emerge. 'It's time to leave', I tell Jesús, 'I'm late for Douglas.' Knowing Douglas, as I do – the shit-stirring little fuck, it won't be long until he's on the phone to my mum, telling her I'm missing and that he's worried about me. Of course it wouldn't be concern, it would be anger that I got a shag and he didn't. If he phones Mum she'll freak. She'll think I've been chopped up into pieces and put in my bum bag. I explain this. Some of this and I'm told –

JESÚS: Soon. We go soon.

ALLY: After lunch we have a siesta and while I'm only too happy to jump back into bed with Jesús, I visualise a press campaign at home, complete with Mother sobbing on *Scotland Today*. *(Beat.)* Siesta's aren't for sleeping by the way, they're the invention of Spanish men, who can't wait for it until bedtime.

ALLY looks up at DELORES.

If it wasn't for afternoon shagging, Delores, I would have left a long time ago. *(Beat.)* Jesús disappears for half an hour and returns with a video of '¿Quién es esa chica?' – Madonna's 'Who's That Girl?' which to this day I've only seen in Spanish, which might be to my advantage. It's not till early evening that we finally get in Roberto's car and leave, and on the drive I convince myself that Mum will have landed at Tenerife airport by now, wearing a black veil. Roberto doesn't take us straight back to town, he stops at a house in the middle of nowhere – Jesús' house – and I'm ushered inside to meet Jesús' mother. Why would I want to meet his mother? Does she know who I am? Does she know her son has given me his gold pendant and several pearl necklaces? Roberto and Jesús disappear to the bedroom, abandoning me in the kitchen with the mother who, transfixed by the television, scarcely looks at me. She pours me a glass of wine and sits me down in front of the *Golden Girls* which has been dubbed into Spanish. And as I watch, my fears about my own mother subside. I begin to enjoy my strange encounter with this enigmatic Spanish woman. And as Blanche, Dorothy, Sofia and Rose gather round the kitchen table at the end of the episode, I realise that they have something I want. And it's not the cheesecake. I realise that I want to be translated too, into Spanish.

ALLY picks up another postcard from the floor and reads it.

I can still taste you. Does the postman read this? Hey postman, I can taste Ally's junk – it's horny! You should try. J.

ALLY rips up the card and goes over to DELORES.

I'm sure all junk tastes the same, Delores. It probably wasn't mine.

DELORES: A man on horseback can go anywhere, and knows how to put pressure on a woman lost in a wasteland.

ALLY: What?

DELORES: Which of us is lost in a wasteland? You or I? Think how many times I've had that man – so many – times when I've wanted him badly, times when I can take him or leave him, times even when I would rather do a crossword. But every time you've had him you've wanted him so badly.

ALLY: Not anymore, Delores.

DELORES: Come on, Ally, it's me you're talking to. You're like parched earth waiting for rain. To be silent and consumed by fire is the worst punishment on earth, we inflict it on ourselves and I pity you. *(Pause.)* You're not leaving. I don't think you should. Even if it means you see him again. It's not a problem to me because at least you...at least you...

DELORES is silent, the light on the picture goes out.

ALLY: At least what, Delores? At least I love him? It might not be a problem to you but...

By the time I have to return to Scotland I've fallen in love with Jesús, who I've seen constantly for the entire holiday. Douglas had to physically drag me away from him, as we said goodbye on the beach. *(Beat.)* On the plane back Douglas tells me that while I was hugging Jesús and snivelling, Jesús was checking out someone else over my shoulder, but I didn't believe him. Back home my broken heart is affecting the way I feel about Scotland. Through my lovesick eyes I can't see any joy or colour in Edinburgh and I long to be back in Tenerife. A few weeks spent pining ends abruptly with a call from Douglas who has been offered a job as a holiday rep in Gran Canaria. He says he can get me a job too. I pack up my life, say goodbye to my mother and go back to the Canary Islands, but not to become a holiday rep and not to have accommodation provided for me, because Douglas lied to get me to go with him. He cheated me into going, duped me into a new life.

ALLY picks up a selection of photographs and cards from the ones on the floor. He holds them up.

These are the 1990s.

ALLY turns the photographs and cards face down and shuffles them.

ALLY: During this decade I'm a barman, a receptionist, a courier, a skinny Pedro-style club rep – a low period, when I want to come back to Scotland but never have quite enough money for the flight. I work for a website, which crashes and burns, I collect money from people lying on dilapidated sun loungers – a job with the fringe benefit that I'm able to speak to every single man, and every non-single man in a square mile of beach. I sell tat on a stall, I work in a hotel – an experience that teaches me to take my own towels on holiday – you would not believe what guests and chamber folk do with towels – sins no boil wash could ever forgive. Then my jobs become sensible, things I could actually put on my CV if I ever return Scotland. I work for an insurance company that celebrates the fact it has never paid a single claim in its existence, I work in a bank, I… I disappear into a monochrome, soft-focus, air-conditioned world of administration. So no wonder my evenings become a little more colourful. No wonder in those ten years I sleep with enough men to populate an area the size of Tunbridge Wells.

ALLY gives the cards one last shuffle, shuts his eyes and pulls out a postcard.

(Reading.) Oh my god, this is insane, what did you do to me? Did you brainwash me – something like Ally Ally I love Ally? I just nearly made a bus crash off the fucking road into the fucking sea. J. *(Putting the postcard back.)* Maybe that would have been better for both of us.

ALLY rips up the card and plucks another from the pack. This one is a photograph. He looks at it.

(Showing the card.) It's me and Douglas in 1993 – our last night out together. We get shitfaced. I'm the kind of dark, reckless drunk I turn into with Douglas. I've pulled this older, muscular guy and we're shagging in his hotel room – I'm on top, giving it big licks – 'STARRING ALLY' – when suddenly something hits me hard in the face. I scream, get off him and go to turn the light on but I can't find the fucking switch. I'm like an insect battering itself against a window trying to get to the… I find it, throw it on and turn to see the guy shaking out his fingers.

– 'Are you not into that?' he says.

– 'No I am fucking not.'

In my pissed state, thinking my words have set things straight, I bang the light off and get back on him. Then a couple of minutes later he punches me again, bursting my nose this time and sending me howling back to the light switch. Fuck the light switch, I grab my shorts off the floor, pull them on and run out of the apartment and out the building. I run down street after street, without stopping or slowing down until I reach the beach. When I reach the sand I lie down and sleep. I wake up early the next morning, cold and jittery. I look down at my T-shirt. The print is obscured by blood. It's the T-shirt I wore to the Bull's Head the night I met Jesús. And I feel like I've spent one long day in the Canary Islands, that starts off in heaven and ends in hell.

ALLY puts the photo back in the pack and shuffles it quickly.

I should have ditched Douglas long before now. He's the bad friend who makes me bad. My self-destructiveness delights him, makes him feel superior, keeps him in fresh gossip.

I pick myself up off the beach and come back to Douglas and my apartment, which is horrible by the way, and smells like a brothel. Douglas is in the kitchen. I stand silently in front of him and he starts to laugh. Which might be OK if he'd sympathised first – given me a hug. But no, he's laughing at me, stood here covered in blood, and he doesn't know what happened. Well he'll never know. I leave him standing in the kitchen, pack my things and move out. And we haven't spoken since. Like I say, that was 1993.

ALLY shuffles the pack. He pulls a photograph out, looks at it, laughs and holds it to his chest.

The backdrop to my 1990s is the Yumbo Centre – a monstrous, concrete shopping centre in the middle of Maspalomas, Gran Canaria. Apparently it's sick now. It has ASR or concrete cancer and will eventually crumble. It's true. I've had more sex in the Yumbo than I have anywhere else – I've done it swinging, standing, in the dark, in the backrooms, in the bars, on the bars, inside, outside, even upside down. Once.

He places the photograph face up on the floor.

This is an ex-boyfriend, Juan. Don Juan de Gran Canaria. We saw each other last in Autumn '96. We met in the Yumbo's famous Thong bar, which boasts the best view in the centre because the staff serve you in flip flops, thongs and nothing else. My barman tonight is Tony. Tony's arse is impressive but his chat, not so much –

TONY: Table for one? We've got a few tables for one in this evening, but that'll all change, believe me. Sit wherever you like, except here *(He points to his face.)* Have you been down the beach today? I love the beach. You know what

I say – life's a beach and then you find one who'll listen to all your problems and go dancing with you. I took my bucket to the beach the other day but you don't want to hear about that, do you? What can I get you?

ALLY: I order a beer and Tony clears the empties off my table. Unable to pick up the last bottle, he performs a well-rehearsed gag of attempting to collect the bottle using his arse cheeks. I am not amused so he sashays away. *(Beat.)* I heard from Don Juan de Gran Canaria recently in an email. He moved to Manchester to do a PhD in something to do with viruses. In the email he told me he had HIV, but not to worry because it's in a test tube, not his bloodstream. He had an unusual sense of humour. While I wait for him, I take in the ghastliness that is the Yumbo, pondering the plastic palm trees and fibreglass dinosaurs that have a certain *Je Ne Sais Quoi*? Or What The Fuck? as we say in English. Across the square, Ricky's Cabaret Bar is waking up. It's the latest addition to the Gran Canaria gay scene – a hybrid of glitter, lip-syncing, and vulgarity, it's about as Spanish as the Bull's Head.

TONY: Look at this – I've never had this before – each of my tables has but one gentleman affiliated to it, with nothing to look at except me. This could make a boy feel self-conscious.

TONY performs a provocative little turn with his tray of drinks to prove that he is in no way self-conscious.

ALLY: When Juan appears I stand up and pull out a chair and at the same time the guys at the other tables do the same.

TONY: What's going on? You can't all leave at once. So, I'm not Ricardo, but what am I, chopped liver?

ALLY: To my horror Juan makes his way around the guys stood by their tables, kissing them on each cheek as he goes before arriving at my table and doing the same to me.

TONY: Oh dear. What's going on here? It looks like someone got his dates muddled. Would you like me to call you a taxi, amigo? Or maybe you should make a run for the fire exit.

ALLY: I shoot an accusatory look at Juan and he responds with a Hispanic shrug.

JUAN: I have something to tell you.

ALLY: He says after a long pause.

JUAN: I have something to tell you all.

TONY: Do you? Surely you've nothing to tell me.

ALLY: Tony has his tray of drinks on one hand above his head, the other hand on his hip and his bottom tilted to one side, looking like it's either asking a question or cheekily mocking us.

JUAN: There is no very easy way to tell you this. I have a dilemma because… I like five guys, I spend a lot of time with each of them and I can't choose.

ALLY: A drink is picked up, emptied over Juan and the perpetrator leaves. We pick up our drinks.

JUAN: Whoa, guys, come on. Don't be like this. You should feel happy – it's hard for me to decide which one of you I like because you're all such nice guys.

ALLY rushes across the room and grabs a mop.

TONY: If anyone else feels moved to throw their drink over this gentleman – and I can't say I blame you if you do – you'll have to clear up after.

ALLY: The other guys down or disregard their drinks and march out leaving me and Juan. I stare into his eyes so intensely I bring tears. He touches me, I recoil, and turn on my heels and ascend the Yumbo staircase in a demonstrative frenzy. At the top of the stairs I look down and Juan is in pursuit of me or one of the others. He's nearly on me when I jump in a taxi and go, never to see him again, never to find out who he would choose, only ever knowing that there was a one in five chance that he wanted to be with me.

ALLY puts the photo of Juan back in the box. He plucks out another and lays it on the floor. It's a photograph of a dog.

This is a dog I spent the night with. I don't know his or her name. It was a one night stand in 1999. By which time I was tiring of island life and losing my patience with the male inhabitants. The dog's owner was called Adam – a barman I thought I'd pulled, who gave me his keys and sent me back to his apartment.

ADAM: When you get back, help yourself to anything, pour yourself a drink. There's porn in the DVD player, get yourself started.

ALLY: I jump up in excitement.

ADAM: And would you mind walking my dog? I'll be another hour or so, and he'll be desperate for a tinkle.

ALLY: A great big squelchy shit more like, that burns my nostrils as I bend down to pick it up from the pavement. I get home and wait for Adam. I watch some porn, the whole film and the extras. I get freaked out by the dog at one point and think it's going to turn on me. But it doesn't, it's a placid creature, that pays me very little attention even when I'm jacking off in front of the movie. I give up on Adam, snuggle in to his dog and fall asleep. Adam staggers in the next morning, heads straight to bed and falls asleep. I throw the dog a ball as hard as I can through the open bedroom door, which has the desired effect on the bouncing, hairy, barking animal. I let myself out.

ALLY shoves the postcard back in the box and opens the laptop – a Gaydar message alert pings. He types.

Yes, I'm still up for it.

He puts down the laptop and exits.

3.

'¿Quien Maneja mi Barca?' *plays and ALLY enters with a vacuum cleaner and starts vacuuming. As he does he dances along to the music, and as the music reaches a crescendo, so does his dancing/vacuuming.*

ALLY: 1983 was my first *Eurovision*. I watched it with Mum, pretending not to be that interested but secretly loving it. I was particularly taken with the Spanish entrant – Maria Delores Amaya Vega or to use her flamenco name Remedios Amaya. She sang '¿Quien Maneja mi Barca?' – 'Who is Sailing My Ship?' I agreed with Mum that Remedios' dress was hideous but I didn't think her performance deserved to get the nul points it eventually scored. I was gutted. I thought she was wonderful – earthy, exotic and somehow vital and I've never been able to get her performance out of my head.

ALLY puts the vacuum cleaner down.

In the year 2000 at the age of thirty I decided to leave Gran Canaria. I'd long been judgemental of men who hang around on the island into their forties, I didn't want to become one so I decided to go.

ALLY collects the rest of the postcards from the floor and puts them in the box.

ALLY: And if I'd gone straight back to Edinburgh…

DELORES: None of this would have happened. You would never have come into our world. We would never have met.

ALLY: We have never met, Delores. *(Beat.)* I went to book my flight at the travel agent, like you did in those days and there was a leaflet on the desk announcing new flights from GC to Tenerife. And my thoughts were immediately of Jesús – the guy I'd been in love with all those years ago. I fantasised about seeing him again. As I gazed at the flyer the fantasy became an impulse and I changed my booking from Scotland to Tenerife. I swap Princes Street in Edinburgh for Playa de Las Americas and I spend a week topping up my tan and buying all the crap I'd spent a decade avoiding. Oh, and I keep an eye out for Jesús but to no avail. On the last night of the hol with maximum tan and a hold-all full of miniature liqueurs I stroll into the Bull's Head. It wasn't that I was saving the best until last, more that I was avoiding the inevitable disappointment. As I walk into the place I feel a pang in my stomach. It hasn't changed at all and what's more, Trish is there, stood behind the bar, with the same perm and in the same blouse she wore ten years previously.

TRISH: I don't remember you, I'm afraid. You must have been here when Terry was still with us, bless him. Remember Terry? Proper piss-taker. He was in the middle of verbally assaulting me when it happened. In fact I was laughing at him as he died. There was nothing I could do to help him – I had four pint glasses in each hand, and by the time I'd put them down and rushed around behind the bar to resuscitate him, he was already gone. A massive heart attack. That's right, Terry had a heart all along. *(TRISH laughs.)* He was a nice man really. I mean he'd say some dreadful things to me, but still he'd do anything for you. Actions speak louder than words, Alistair. Actions speak louder than words. Terry lived by that – it was his motto.

ALLY: I tell her I'm leaving Gran Canaria. She asks why? I don't know what to say. I tell her something lame about various heartaches and disappointments. And I tell her I'm getting old. Which she laughs at, she says I'm just a boy. For some reason I tell her about Don Juan de Gran Canaria, as though he has anything to do with anything. I hear myself saying all this crap I didn't plan to say and I sound broken, bitter, pathetic.

TRISH: I hope you're tougher than that, Alistair. You can't crumble when the first two-timing sod does the dirty on you.

ALLY: 'He was five-timing me,' I say, shocked that it's still raw after all this time.

TRISH: You need to ask yourself why you really want to leave Gran Canaria. Be honest with yourself. What did you come out here for? What did you want to achieve? Have you achieved it?

ALLY: I don't really know. I wanted to party I guess. I've done that. I wanted to be the centre of attention. I have been. And to have an adventure, and stories to tell. *(Beat.)* But I really wanted my life to be un film de Pedro Almodóvar, to be translated into Spanish. I wanted to escape the fake plastic trees of the Yumbo Centre and to live in Madrid. But in ten years on the island I've hardly picked up a word of Spanish and I wouldn't know where to start in Madrid or Barcelona. Just then my unexpected therapy session, fuelled by a few generous somethings and Coke, brings to my lips a name, and that name is Remedios Amaya.

TRISH: Never heard of her.

ALLY: She's the 1983 Eurovision entrant for Spain.

TRISH: I'm not into all that shit. Terry was. That's one thing I really don't miss about him, god rest his soul.

ALLY: I ask Trish if she's heard of Ricky's Cabaret Bar.

TRISH: I went there once, it was shit. If I wanted to spend an evening having the shit ripped out of me by a man that thinks he's hilarious, I would have stayed in Tenerife.

ALLY: 'I want to take Remedios to Ricky's, Trish.' I tell her as though it had ever previously crossed my mind to do so, which I can assure you it hasn't.

TRISH: Well you should and you will. You must. *(Beat.)* I want you to promise you will.

ALLY: I say nothing.

TRISH: Promise me, Alistair, you'll get up there and show those drag queens a thing or two.

ALLY: So I say, 'Yes, OK, I will. I promise.' And that's it. That's how this happened. A drunken promise to a woman I may never see again. It's the only commitment I have in my life so I keep it.

ALLY goes over to the photo of DELORES.

That's how it happened, Delores. That's why I met him.

DELORES: Bull shit.

ALLY opens the suitcase and takes out a hideous blue and white striped dress.

Ricky's Cabaret Bar is owned and run by a little fat drag queen called Davina Divine – Dave to his friends. The night after I get back from Tenerife, with a few cocktails under my belt, I slip into Ricky's and perch at one of the tables in the back corner. Dave is doing a set.

DAVE: What are you lot doing here at this time of year? It's fucking dead. Sitges – that's where you want to be. Gran Canaria's deserted. You lot must all be chasing after the same fucking guy. And if there's so much as one bloke on this island worth chasing after, I haven't seen him. I was down at rudey nudie the other day. You know what I'm talking about – I mean the gay beach. It were like Dad's Army had stripped off and gone for their nana nap. I was lying there myself – lovely image I know. I'd forgotten I was naked – couldn't see my manhood for my tits and belly. I see something pert on the horizon and think, thank god someone round here has got an arse worth looking at – but it turns out two dykes are throwing a beach ball back and forward to each other. I mean it's a sorry state of affairs when you're lusting after inflatables. OK, well since this looks like all we're going to get this evening by way of an audience, myself, the lovely Gina G-spot and the marvellous Miss Demeanour are going to get started. So turn your hearing aids to the Tranny position – and give it up for 'Oops! I Did It Again'.

'Oops! I Did It Again' *plays and DAVE walks off stage.*

ALLY: After 'Oops! I Did It Again', Dave goes over and sits at the bar. I approach him, I seem suspicious, like I'm soliciting the services of a private detective. I sit by him and blurt out that I'd like to try out my Remedios Amaya. Dave gives me a long hard stare. Excruciatingly long.

DAVE: You what?

ALLY: I start to repeat myself.

DAVE: I heard what you said. I just don't know what to say. I thought you worked in an office. If I had a proper job I wouldn't be doing this, believe me. I've got friends who work in the West End. Of London. If they could see me now, they'd wet their knickers.

ALLY: I tell Dave about Remedios and her Eurovision entry –

DAVE: Gina G-spot did a one man-woman Eurovision mega mix a couple of years back, called Water-LuLu. I was defeated. I got Nul Points. It didn't go down very well. But since everyone's in Sitges at the moment and you can't do too much damage, I'm happy to try you out, Ally. Well, happy is maybe a strong word, but you're booked, you're on next Tuesday. If it's dreadful, you'll know about it – you won't get a second chance.

ALLY holds up the dress.

A neighbour made this for me from some curtain material I bought in Las Palmas. It's arguably even uglier than the original.

Tuesday night arrives, as do I, by taxi to the Yumbo centre. Unfortunately this curtain material is incredibly hot, itchy and not designed for skin contact.

In my nervous state the next hour jitters by quickly, and suddenly I'm on the stage at Ricky's, stood in front of the small crowd. Only now do I realise they'll think my feet are bare because I'm new to this and haven't found any size ten ladies shoes. But my feet are bare because Remedios' feet were bare – her dress being too hideous to find shoes to match it.

DELORES is illuminated and ALLY turns to look at her.

DELORES: This is how he sees you for the first time, dressed like this – a hideous mockery of a real woman.

The light fades on DELORES.

ALLY: It's the first time anyone has seen me like this. But it wasn't the first time he saw me. It was maybe the first time he noticed me properly since I'm not sat behind a desk, peering at him through a stack of in-trays.

In Munich, in 1983, Remedios Amaya was the 7th act to take to the stage for the 28th Eurovision song contest. As she stood in front of her audience she looked worried and alone. I feel her loneliness as I stand, nearly two decades later before a far smaller crowd. The song begins with terrifying thumps and strangulated howling wind instruments of some variety. It sounds as though a high speed train is going to soar across the stage and take Remedios with it. This might be to her advantage. Remedios looks down at her dress, as though she's just realised what the fuck she's wearing and has quickly considered a last minute change. But there's no time for that, she has questions to ask. One question in particular, that she asks a total of eighteen times – 'Who is sailing my boat? Who is sailing my boat? Who is sailing my boat?' There are other things she'd like to know too, she wants to know – 'Your mother's braids, come on, tell me who. Tell me who braids them, tell me who, tell me who.' This obscure question is the last one I lip-sync to before my mouth refuses to go on. My lips and jaw become slack, I break sweat and look at the audience with terror in my eyes – oh shit, I'm going to get the same nul points she did. Remedios continues caterwauling courageously but I'm silent, sweating and swaying. I motion with my hand to cut the music, but as I do I see him – José. He works for the same company as me and once in a blue moon he works in my office. And he's heart-stoppingly handsome, and he has the most wonderful smile and he's smiling now, and he's the straightest, most earthy, wholesome, relaxed, masculine, Spanish man. And why on earth is he sitting in Ricky's? And how come he's in Ricky's tonight, when I am dressed in a diagonally striped shroud, mouthing an authentic flamenco song at a room full of people who would all far rather I, or someone else, was singing 'Hit Me Baby One More Time'? Gina G-spot presses 'stop' on the CD and I leave the stage. The sound of sustained microphone feedback as I flee backstage is real or imaginary but it's definitely there. There is no applause. I look at myself in the mirror and say – 'It's time to leave GC. We're leaving tomorrow.' I hide backstage until several acts have passed. And while I sit there sweating I realise I've finally done it – I've forced myself off the island. I've deliberately burned my bridges. Dave eventually comes in bearing a small bucket of vodka and coke.

DAVE: What happened, love? Are you feeling alright, I haven't seen anything that uncomfortable since Lady Large had her funny turn. And even then she was still in tune, even after she vomited blood on herself. Would you like a drink?

ALLY: I nod slowly and seriously without looking at Dave.

DAVE: I'm afraid to leave you on your own in here in case you hang yourself. I know I would.

ALLY: I get rid of the dress, down the drink and emerge into the bar.

ALLY puts the dress in the suitcase.

Fortunately, while I've been backstage, the clientele has turned over considerably and as I come out I get nothing more than a couple of odd looks. I crash at the nearest table. José stands over me.

JOSÉ: That was strange. *(Beat.)* I can join you?

ALLY: He sits down. I ask him what he's doing in here.

JOSÉ: Don't tell anyone.

ALLY: Don't tell anyone! Oh my god, José is gay! I tell him I'm not a drag queen, and I don't normally do this kind of thing. 'What are you doing here?' – I ask again.

JOSÉ: Drinking.

ALLY: He winks at me. Actually winks. Oh my god, I'm going to shag José. But he's married. I know this, I asked someone at work. He's married with children. He's born and bred Canarian. He used to be a party boy, now he's a family man. He lives in Las Palmas de Gran Canaria. He's an IT engineer. He travels around the island fixing people's computers. He drains his glass, stands, and waits for me to do the same, which I do and we leave, get a taxi, go to his hotel room and… I'm in José's fucking hotel room. He strips off, waits for me to undress and then he kisses me, puts his hands all over me. In the future when I feel his hands all over me I think of the first time his hands were all over me and – these are fucking José's hands – and they're all over my arse and he's eating my face and I cannot fucking believe this. And this is the best sex I have ever had. I don't sleep I just make love to José until he sleeps and then I lie staring at him. When he wakes the next morning the sex is even better and I fall in love with him. Just like that. Like someone has thrown a rock into my stomach. And I realise I have been in love with him since I first set eyes on him –

DELORES: Stop it, Ally, I'm going to puke! It's not love you feel, it's lust. The man you think you'll never have gives you a little fuck and you think a lightning bolt has hit you between the eyes? Get a grip. You know he has a wife. You should have had a nice night… Yes let him take you in the morning, but then leave him and keep a happy memory.

ALLY: He gets up to leave. He doesn't shower, he just gets dressed. And I ask him when I will see him again and he laughs. He doesn't give me his phone number, he just goes, leaves me with my thoughts. And although I'm confused, I feel incredible and I realise that there are things out there that are good and that can make you happy and that sex can be great and that love exists. And fuck Scotland, I'm going nowhere. I might have as little security today as I did yesterday, but for the first time on this island, I have hope. And even though José has a wife…

ALLY goes over to the photo of DELORES.

This is her. This is Delores. She's beautiful. He loves her, he tells me, and I believe him. What's not to love? José knows I have this.

DELORES: And how long does this last?

ALLY: For ten years.

DELORES: I mean how long does this silly feeling last. This silly honeymoon period, when you can't eat, you can't think straight, you have thoughts in your head that would make me want to vomit?

ALLY takes the picture of DELORES off the wall and puts it on top of the suitcase.

ALLY: My father passed away in 2001, a few weeks after the night of Remedios/José. A few weeks after the night I died on stage in the Yumbo and came back to life in José's hotel room. I went back for the funeral. For one day. Makes me feel sick thinking about it. Mum wanted me to stay for a week at least. She wanted her son there. I lied to her. Said I had work, said the only flights I could afford were…I lied. And those lies are the reason I can't return to Scotland. Because there's nowhere in Edinburgh I can hide from the fact I rejected my mother when she needed me most. I'd made my bed in Spain and I had to lie in it. For months I'm in solitary confinement, sitting in here, whenever I'm not at work, in case he comes round. Not knowing, when that will be, if ever. Realising that the man I love is impossible to pin down.

DELORES: I've already pinned him down. I've got the ring to prove it, and the house, and the children and the long silent nights when I'm with him but have no use for him. When I have how you say…Tengo dolor de cabeza?

ALLY: I have a headache. *(Beat.)* The honeymoon feeling lasts for years, until 2004, or 2005, but it doesn't seem that long. Because during those years I'm only alive for twenty-six days, the twenty-six days we're together.

DELORES: Twenty-six days to save a marriage. Twenty-six days of giving José what I can't and filling the gap between us. Twenty-six days of sticking it in another man is a small price to pay for a happy home, happy husband, children who don't have their father leave and become a faggot.

ALLY: 'Would you ever leave Delores for me?' He doesn't respond for about a minute. The question is a long time coming. It's 2005, the affair's about to go into its fifth year but it still feels fragile. And I feel like the words feel powerful, like they could blow me out to sea, never to return.

JOSÉ: You don't want a faggot, Ally. You gave up on them a long time ago. You want a José, you get a Delores too.

ALLY: And that's all he says on the matter. And the next time I see him.

DELORES: You get a Delores.

ALLY: We're in a hotel room in Las Palmas de Gran Canaria. It's the only time I ever go to see him rather than the other way around, the only time I ever see José looking uncomfortable. The only time it's ever complicated, so I never go again.

JOSÉ: Delores is a kilometre from here. I don't like it.

ALLY: I ask him what Delores looks like. He shows me this photograph.

JOSÉ: Keep it.

ALLY: He says. I ask why, but he doesn't answer me and I keep it. And I will never know why he has given it to me. I guess because if I want a José I have to have a Delores too. *(Beat.)* Delores and I have been talking a lot about José lately, but it's not always like this. We talk about everything. We talk about her children, we talk about my work – she likes to gossip about my colleagues. I never think, I've got your man, or if only you knew what I have in my bed.

DELORES: Of course I knew something was going on. I knew since the start. Suddenly José is more perky, more working away a lot and more humming the songs of Steps and Madonna. But he's still turning up for his marriage and he's still a good father to his children, who adore their Daddy.

ALLY puts the photo of DELORES in the suitcase. He goes to the wall and takes down a photo of a barman.

ALLY: It's the winter of 2007, I've been sleeping with José for six years. I'm sitting in Cockring bar. When I came to GC, the gays came to the island because it was a safer place to be gay, but by now it's safe everywhere so it's changed, it's become a place to get down and dirty. And Cockring is as dirty as the name suggests. I've not seen or heard from José for over a month. This is nothing new, he never phones me, he either sends me a postcard, instructing me where to meet him or he turns up at my apartment. The longest I've had to go without a postcard or a visit was eleven weeks in 2006 which was tough. Sometimes I think I can live like this – I accept that if I want to have a José I have to live with this uncertainty, other times it's just a head-fuck. When it becomes too much of a head-fuck I pack my bags to leave but whenever I do he turns up.

DELORES: I am in and out of a suitcase more times than the stockings of an air hostess. Where are we going this time, Ally? You want to take me to Manchester? You say it's like Gran Canaria without the sun, plonked in the middle of a post-industrial metropolis?

ALLY: We're going nowhere in Britain, Delores. *(Beat.)* It's 2007 and I'm sat at the bar in Cockring. I think I saw José's car in town this afternoon. I've convinced myself I did – he's come to Maspalomas but not to see Ally. The one thing I've pinned him down about is that if he starts sleeping with other men, it's over. I'm in Cockring, as a spy, and if José walks in here, I'll kill him. I'm talking to the barman. Telling him about José. This is significant as it's the first time I've talked to anyone apart from Delores about him.

SANDY: You should sack him off, Ally, he's using you. He doesn't know who he is so let him go. After six years with a guy you should have a house together, or a dog, or at least a half-decent coffee maker. You don't even have his phone number? Listen, the bird in the hand is worth two in the bush and yours is spending way too much time in the bush.

ALLY: I tell the barman, I love him. José that is. I tell him that every time I try to leave, José turns up or I get a postcard and I stay and I wait for one more time.

SANDY: Does he love you?

ALLY: I don't know the answer. José has never said.

ALLY takes a postcard from the box

(Reading.) I break the rules. Forgive me. Only to say you're very special to me. I don't want it to be the end. I want to make it better. I write again very soon. Go nowhere. J.

ALLY rips it up and throws the pieces on the ground.

If you can't leave on a high you should cut your losses and leave with an element of dignity. Something Remedios and I have always struggled to do. Towards the end of her Eurovision ordeal, realising how badly she was doing, Remedios frantically covered the stage, striding around, searching for a sympathetic pocket of audience, whilst at the same time chastising the onlookers with disapproving finger waving. And as the song finally came to an end she proudly struck a defiant pose and shrieked the song's final 'who'. *(Beat.)* José never came into Cockring and I never asked him if he loved me. Not until 2010 anyway, eight years after I took Remedios to Ricky's.

JOSÉ: You can't have my image.

ALLY: José says to me. We're lying next to each other on the gay beach. And I know why he says this but I'm angry. Why can't I be trusted with the photograph of a man I've been with for so long? 'Do you love me, José?' I ask loudly, I've finally found my voice and it's direct, it has a bit of a growl in it.

JOSÉ: You know you can't have my photograph.

ALLY: I said, do you love me?

JOSÉ: A little bit.

ALLY: He replies. And with his little bit of love he stabs me in the chest. A little bit? This is when I realise that I'm not his lover, just an eight year fuck buddy.

ALLY puts the box of cards and photographs in the suitcase. He takes down the remaining photos and packs them also. Finally he puts the photograph of DELORES in and he shuts the case.

José is coming here tomorrow night. I will have left. There will be no note and no number. He'll never find me. I'll be dead to him. It's his turn to wonder, to guess and to be kept in the dark. When he gets here, there will be nothing except…

ALLY opens the laptop.

37

(Typing.) Where are you? *(Beat.)* He will unlock the door and there will be nothing here except...

A Gaydar message alert sounds. ALLY reads the message.

The smell of Canarian Boy 1985 WE.

He shuts the laptop and puts it in the suitcase. The apartment is empty.

It's last Friday. I'm sitting watching the door, waiting to hear José's key in the lock. He has his own key but I don't even have his phone number. I've been sitting here for hours. I've been here before, many times, and I decide that this is the last time and that I will actually leave this time. I'm going to go to Madrid, to real Spain. I'm going to start a real life and if I meet anyone who has a wife, or is a weirdo, or who talks shit to me, or isn't available, I'm going to turn around and walk away.

The flat buzzer sounds. ALLY goes over and picks up the receiver.

I'm forty-two years old, I have a wealth of experience, I've been lied to, cheated on, humiliated, loved, adored, dumped and duped. I have photographs older than you. I am going to Madrid this evening and I won't be back, so don't get attached. If you're still up for it, come up, if you're not, you're not – you can't upset or offend me.

He presses the door release.

Next Spring I'll be in Madrid. *(Beat.)* I'll be sitting outside a café and I'll order un cortado, por favor. A man in a smart black suit will walk over and sit at a nearby table. He will look like José and I'll stare at him. Catching me staring he'll smile. He'll ask to read my paper and I'll give it to him. He'll read for a minute, and then spark up conversation with me. There's a play he wants to see at the theatre and he'll tell me about it. I'll tell him it sounds interesting. He'll say I should go with him. I won't trust him at first, I'll see Juan, Jesús and José. Then when he writes his number on a piece of paper and hands it to me it will be like I've waited a decade for this moment. And as I fold the piece of paper and put it in my wallet, twenty years on the Canary Islands will become so small it could fit on the back of a postcard.

The doorbell rings. ALLY goes to the door and puts his hand on the handle. He opens the door.

Blackout.

The End.

I HEART MATHS

I Heart Maths was initially developed by Glasgay!, Ros Philips and students of the MA Classical and Contemporary Text and BA Acting courses at RSAMD.

I Heart Maths was first performed on Monday, 23 May 2011 for A Play, A Pie and A Pint at Òran Mór, Glasgow.

CAST

BRIAN and BARMAN, Michael Gray

ALISON and JOHN, Isabelle Joss

MICHAEL, Matthew McVarish

CREW

Directed by, Ros Philips

Technicians,   Andrew Cowan
               Gary Wilson
               Ross Kirkland
               Niall McMenimen

Sound Designer, Danny Krass

Stage Manager, Andy Dempsey

Designer, Patrick McGurn

Assistant Designer, Kirsten Hogg

Trainee Producer, Sarah Macfarlane

Associate Producer, Susannah Armitage

Producer, David Maclennan

Characters

MICHAEL
A lecturer

ALISON
Michael's colleague

BRIAN
Michael's student

JOHN
Daphne's Bar barman

(The actor who plays the part of ALISON also plays the part of JOHN.)

A packed lecture theatre. MICHAEL stands at the whiteboard writing the following words/equations – 'Derivations', 'Deleterious' 'Ploidy', 'Monoploid number', 'X = n = 23', 'Mutation Selection Balance'.

MICHAEL: *(Turning to the class.)* Bio-mathematicians. Third years. Fellow adults. Those who have given up growing marijuana and now grow beards, consult IFAs and spend your student loans on buy-to-let mortgages. You no longer drink on a Monday night and prefer a Soy Chai Latté and a flick through *The Independent.* I think you're ready for a challenge. *(Beat.)* Derivations, anyone? What's that doing up there? Where did it come from? Deleterious – just a poncey word for harmful. Can also mean subversive. Bio-mathematics is so subversive. Ploidy – possibly the best word in the English language – just means the number of sets of chromosomes in a biological cell. From it we get the haploid number, n, and the monoploid number, x. Who can tell me about $x = n = 23$? What does it express? Is it an energy drink? A new bar on the south side? *(Beat.)* Anyone?

BRIAN rushes in and sits down.

BRIAN: $X = n = 23 = Man$.

MICHAEL: And the slightly more modern collective term for Man is?

BRIAN: Humans. I meant humans.

MICHAEL: Thank you. Brian's right. Late as usual, but right. $X = n = 23 = Man$ or to give us our post 19th-century title, the human being. Now, you'll have realised by now that you have to do an awful lot of maths before you get to the sexy stuff but d'you know what, I think we've arrived. We're in the mathematic bedroom. And we're finally rid of the bimbos, the dimbos, the Oxbridge rejects, the trust fund timewasters, the far-too-pissed-even-by-academic-standards. The am drams, the unplanned prams, the random woman who changed to nursery nursing, the guy with the gun, that girl, Jennifer, who had all those accidents in the first year – god rest her soul – and of course the dearly deported. Because although education might seem like a good way to escape a life of poverty and persecution, the fees can be a bit prohibitive. Anyway, it's time for me to share what is unquestionably the most important principle in the field of mathematical probability. Sadly, it can also be a little depressing. It's the reason that several of you have to do re-sits. It's why I've just taken rather a lot of time off work to recover from the shock of arriving home one evening and finding someone who wasn't supposed to be in my bedroom, in my bedroom – And I don't mean a burglar. I mean an additional person to Adam was there. I mean Adam was shagging someone else. In my bed. I mean shit happens. Or haploids, as we might say when speaking in terms of chromosomes. That's a little bio-mathematic joke for you. Because shit happens we can try to work out when, why and how shit doesn't happen. We can take the shit, and make something out of it. *(Beat.)* Does anybody have any questions? *(Beat.)* I do. I want to know why. I'm not doing all this maths for the fun of it. I'm not Carol Vorderman. Of course you'll have heard me quote, many times, The Count from *Sesame Street*, with the words 'Ha, ha, ha, I love counting!' But things have happened lately that mean I can't say that. I just can't. *(Pause.)* For this, and various other reasons, I have initiated a research project to discover why my $x = n = 23$ human being was a cheat. I want to find a way of steering clear of mutated relationships in the future. Obviously the University of Manchester won't be funding this particular study which is why, I'm afraid, I'm leaving the faculty. You will have a shiny new lecturer from Monday, who isn't falling apart at the seams.*(Beat.)* Now, I feel like I'm breaking up with you. I suppose I am. *(Grabbing his briefcase.)* I'm no good at goodbyes. Good luck.

MICHAEL darts out of the lecture theatre.

2.

Later the same day. MICHAEL and ALISON in a café.

ALISON: The Dean knows something's going on, Michael, and
I can't keep pretending to be you, or to have seen you.
She keeps catching me in your lecture theatre after *your*
lectures. Yesterday, I had to pretend I'd gone in to wash
your mug up. What kind of feminist must she think I am?
I lowered the pitch of my voice for a whole lecture the
other day in case she heard me through the door. I
practically gave myself laryngitis. This can't go on. *(Beat.)*
Tell her you were pished, that you were speaking shite to
your students and it won't happen again. *(Pause.)*
I invited you for a drink the day we met and you turned
me down. Remember? At the time, I didn't know if you
were socially awkward, a prick or a socially awkward
prick. But I assumed you'd had a better offer. I mean we
were surrounded by cute young gay guys. I was the only
cute youngish gay girl. I thought great, he's got his…
community, I've got my bottle of wine at home, so off I
fucked, alone. But when I got home I had to turn around
because I'd forgotten my diary.

MICHAEL: Not like you to err, Alison.

ALISON: Er, no, it's not. I hated myself. How could I be so
careless with all my life data? I had a lot to deal with that
day – rejection and loss.

MICHAEL: Rejection from a stranger and the loss of a diary?

ALISON: Rejection from a maths genius.

MICHAEL: Shut up.

ALISON: You don't deserve to be so talented. You should have
been stupid. *(Beat.)* I got to uni and found it. And I found
you, stood at the blackboard, hand in pocket of creepy,
polyester maths teacher trousers – the like of which I have
never seen since, thank God. That was back before you
started your gym-squats regime so your bottom looked

a little bit sad. The instant I saw you, I knew why you'd turned me down, and I admired you for it. You were on a date – with maths. Don't be embarrassed, Michael. We're all the same. All academics are in love with the romance of standing at a lectern in a crumbling old university building and there's nothing vain about dressing appropriately. I dress differently depending on which theatre I'm in. I find that dogtooth works well with mahogany but looks horrendous in a modernist concrete cube, and incidentally so does white. I made that mistake once before. I was like a floating head.

MICHAEL: I always wear tweed in the old building. It must be the wood panels.

ALISON: Of course it's the bloody wood panels. Make you feel sexy, don't they? They do me. They're just about the only thing that do.

BRIAN appears by the table. ALISON looks up.

ALISON: Why are you looming over me? Can't you see I'm getting hysterical? Do I look like I might need *more* coffee? *(Beat.)* We'll just have the bill.

BRIAN: Michael, you're making a mistake. If you leave… The other lecturer is good, but –

MICHAEL: Brian, this is Alison.

ALISON: I'm the other lecturer.

BRIAN: Oh. Shit. So you fucking are.

MICHAEL: Alison changes the way she appears to us according to her surroundings.

BRIAN: Cool. You're polymorphic.

ALISON: Am I fuck polymorphic. Thanks for your comments. We'll see you when we're next financially obligated to.

BRIAN: I meant to say the other lecturer's great –

ALISON: Great, but she doesn't keep you awake at night?

BRIAN: Michael, I know your ex-boyfriend hurt you but –

ALISON: Forget his ex-boyfriend. Forget everything he said. He was drunk. He's got a drink problem, okay? That's all. He's fine now. Look – he's back on the hot chocolate. If you must know he's just been wrestling with some… existentialist angst. It's a gay thing. It comes to you all. He'll be back. You won't have to suffer the other lecturer. But try to keep your eyes on the sums, not on the buns, okay? You'll learn more that way. Probably. Thanks for saying hello. It's been nice talking to you. Goodbye.

BRIAN exits.

ALISON: You've hit self-destruct, Michael. What's next? Are you going to expose yourself further? Why don't you just hang out with your wang out?

MICHAEL: I came back to work thinking it would make me happy, but. It's meaningless. It's just numbers.

ALISON: It's all just numbers. We're just numbers. Calculations.

MICHAEL: I want out of my PhD, Alison. I want to help people.

ALISON: You're depressed. Depression makes you want to help people. You should help yourself.

MICHAEL: I have a theory. *(Beat.)* What Adam did can be explained by an external force.

ALISON: The person he was shagging?

MICHAEL: No. He was responding to an instinct because he didn't have –

ALISON: Morals?

MICHAEL: Why does everyone think that gay men don't have morals? Morals are just cultural values which are as diverse as cultural groups. Gay men are actually incredibly moral, in that they are consistently true to their cultural values.

ALISON: You're all slags – is that what you mean?

MICHAEL: No. Adam behaved like a slag because he didn't know that he was meant to be with me. He didn't realise our relationship was the frontier of our individual evolutions and that –

ALISON: He knew fine well he was doing. He thought I'm meant to be with Michael but I want to sit on that, so fuck it, fuck Michael. I'm sorry, Michael, but that's the kind of person he is.

MICHAEL: Adam is lost and searching.

ALISON: Yes, and he's finding, someone else every night. Adam, at the pinnacle of evolution? That's not the kind of pinnacles Adam's interested in.

MICHAEL: If Adam was faced with the precarious mathematics involved in us finding each other he'd behave differently. If I can explain to him that we have reached this equilibrium frequency for a reason and that for this delicate balance to be maintained we need to…

ALISON: What?

MICHAEL: I don't know. Yet. It's all very well knowing how to express the fitnesses of male genotypes comparing straight and gay allele but what I need is time to conduct a Darwinian style study of the gay village.

ALISON: Well there are plenty of primates on Canal Street. They'll not take kindly to you turning up in your safari gear, taking photos though. *(Beat.)* Actually, they'd probably like that, wouldn't they? This is a joke, right?

MICHAEL: I believe that in order for the human race to survive as a species, nature has created a deluge of attraction, in the same way it has created a deluge of –

ALISON: Mosquitoes, maggots, viruses, seagulls, rats,
pigeons…I don't believe in a grand design.

MICHAEL: A deluge of everything has been created. All
possible combinations of sexual attraction are present in
the human race to ensure the survival of the entire species.

ALISON: I have a question for you. So fucking what?

MICHAEL: So, Adam isn't off doing something that has
nothing to do with the rest of society. He's part of the glue
that's holding the species together.

ALISON: And you think if you can prove that, he'll want to get
back with you? *(Beat.) (In hushed tones.)* Listen, Michael.
I don't have a girlfriend. I'm like you were before you
met Adam. I've got maths, I've got money, I've got coffee
shops, shopping shops, a documentary about Henry
Stephen Smith, the father of pure mathematics at eight
o'clock on BBC four, which I'm not missing. I have nice
clothes that co-ordinate with different lecture theatres, I
make simple tasty dishes for one, I have occasional nights
of passion with boyish girls I meet in places like this, which
is the reason I'm whispering. Life is great. Fantastic. But
if you ask me what it means… I wouldn't have a fucking
clue. *(Beat.)* Don't give up on doctor because mister and
mister didn't work out. I'm away to watch my programme.

ALISON stands.

MICHAEL: I'm going to head into The Village.

ALISON: To study the primates? Why don't you just go and
have a good time. Get drunk, embrace promiscuity. And
come to work tomorrow.

MICHAEL: I'll see how I feel.

ALISON: Well, I'm not covering for you anymore.

ALISON exits.

3.

Later the same night in a packed bar. Very loud music. MICHAEL is swaying, holding a drink and intermittently trying to hide his face while he talks to an unseen man.

MICHAEL: *(Shouting over music.)* I'm a mathemagician. I'm a mathemagician. Mathagician. I'm a maths teacher. I'm doing a peee aitch deee. Don't wanna talk about it though. Blah. Yuck. Wish I was a magician. Wish I had a magic wand. I'm teeeeching at the university of manchest-arse. Man chest arse. Man chest arse. Do you know suggestive probably? Suggestive probably. Can't even speak. Subjective probability, know it? No? Piece of piss. Do it standing on my head. Apply it to everything. Shove it up your arse if you like – can make you a very rich man. Not me. Not a gambler. What are the chances of meeting someone... Someone who's field of mathamadic's subjective prob-a-bil-i-tea? What are the chances of meeting a mathemagician full stop? What are the chances of talking to a nice man like you? What's the bet you gotta a boyfriend? You gotta boyfriend? Fucking knew it. I just had to prove it. That's the way it always is every time, know what I mean? You know it but you just gotta prove it. Know what I mean? That's where madamagic comes in. That's where madamagic comes into the equation. *(Pause.)* That's it! *(Beat.)* Fucking prove it. Use the madamagic to prove the fucking theory. Abracadabra, pif pof poof. I don't mean you. You're lovely. Where's your boyfriend gone to? If he's not your boyfriend, whatcha waiting for, call a taxi. What are the chances? Call me a taxi. I'm a taxi. The more the fucking merrier. Led's go!

MICHAEL stumbles out.

4.

MICHAEL's bedroom the next morning. MICHAEL sits up in bed.

MICHAEL: This is brilliant. I don't need to drop out of my PhD. I can prove it mathematically. I can create a genetic model for homosexuality generating testable predictions.

JOHN's head emerges from the covers.

JOHN: Are you still pissed?

MICHAEL: Adam is meant to be with me and I can prove it. Homosexuality has its roots in the evolution of the species, Adam is my perfect fittest partner and I can prove it all with Mathematics. Alison's going to be so happy.

JOHN: Is Alison your wife?

MICHAEL: No. Alison's –

BRIAN tumbles out the bottom of the bed.

BRIAN: She's the other lecturer.

MICHAEL: What the fuck! Brian?! What's he doing here?

JOHN: What d'you think he's doing here? You dragged us into the taxi. You're lucky no one else wanted to come.

MICHAEL: Oh my God did anyone see us?

BRIAN: No. There was no one there but a load of total dogs. *(Beat.)* Present company excluded.

MICHAEL: Brian, please tell me we didn't shag?

JOHN: Don't worry. You pulled out.

MICHAEL: What? I pulled out or I pulled out?

JOHN: Relax. You've still got your jeans on. You didn't do any sex with anyone. You passed out as soon as you walked in the door. I thought you'd brought us to Emily Bishop's house by mistake.

MICHAEL: You have to go, Brian.

BRIAN scrabbles around for his clothes.

JOHN: You could at least give the boy a brew before you turf him out on his arse.

MICHAEL: Do you want a drink, Brian?

BRIAN: I wouldn't mind a coffee.

JOHN: I'll have a gin and tonic.

MICHAEL: Just now?

JOHN: Do you feel you're in the position to comment on my lifestyle?

MICHAEL: I don't have any gin.

JOHN: What you got?

MICHAEL: Red wine. I think.

JOHN: Then that'll have to do. Ice and a slice.

MICHAEL exits.

JOHN: *(To BRIAN who is sitting on the floor.)* Do you want to come to me or shall I come to you?

BRIAN gets into bed beside JOHN.

JOHN: It's a bit funny that this guy hasn't got any poppers?

BRIAN: I guess.

JOHN: I've got poppers at my place.

BRIAN: So? Do you think I'm going to run around to your place and bounce about on your cock because you've got a bottle of poppers?

JOHN: Yes.

BRIAN feels around underneath the covers.

BRIAN: You've got one of those ones that's practically the same size whichever mood it's in. Good for the changing room at the gym. I wish I had one. Of my own I mean.

BRIAN pulls his hand away from JOHN and sits up.

BRIAN: I really like this guy.

JOHN: Pity.

BRIAN: How's it a pity?

JOHN: He's just not that in to you.

MICHAEL comes in with the coffee and the wine.

JOHN: *(Taking his wine.)* Thanks. I'm off work tonight so I may as well keep going. As a publican I find – watching pissed folk all the time – when I'm off work I want to get at least as twatted as my customers. Well, not to the point when I'm actually sick on myself. Have you been to Daphne's?

MICHAEL: No.

BRIAN: Where did you and Adam live?

MICHAEL: Deansgate. Number one.

JOHN: I knew a queen who lived on Deansgate. She was always hanging off her balcony looking for rent. She was a lawyer. Thought she was Posh Spice. Thought she could find herself a footballer. She did eventually, but she had to pay him almost as much as a real one to get him to stay the night. She just wanted to be a wag. Slag. *(Beat.)* I'm near Deansgate. I'm at Fairy Towers. That's where me and Brian are going in a bit.

BRIAN: Are we?

JOHN: Yes. Einstein has to get started on his…what is it?

MICHAEL: I'm making a…gayness model that generates testable predictions.

BRIAN: How?

JOHN: What?

MICHAEL: These are both good questions. I look at large biological processes and I work out a way to simulate them mathematically. So I make an equation with variables of all the different things going on in any biological process. Now that can be something really small, like the operation of one part of a cell or it could be really big, like all the functions of a group of people. Now, you know Darwin?

BRIAN: Yes.

JOHN: No. *(Beat.)* Wait, who's the one in the wheelchair, bless him?

BRIAN: Stephen Hawking?

JOHN: That's the one. I often think with science, people just do anything out of curiosity without working out why they want to do it. It's like we managed to put a man on the moon. Hooray, let's stick a flag in it. And then you're like – why? *(Beat.)* Where are you doing your research? You should come to Daphne's. My bar. Good old-fashioned gay boozer – trannies and everything. The customers will do anything for cash. Or you could always come to Fairy Towers. My home. The whole tower is filled with queens. Like anywhere it has its ups and downs. On the one hand there's a high crime rate, on the other hand most of them are non-violent. On the downside there's a lot of unemployment, on the bright side recreational drugs are easy to get hold of. And while it's a pain in the neck the lifts never work, you get to meet more folk when you take the stairs.

JOHN drains his glass. He gets out of bed and drags BRIAN out too. They dress.

JOHN: Thanks for the hospitality. Pop into Daphne's anytime. Say hello. And if you do want to go to Fairy Towers, we're all very accommodating. You don't even have to knock.

JOHN goes to the door. BRIAN stands, looking at MICHAEL.

JOHN: Come on, you.

JOHN exits. BRIAN follows him.

5.

Later that day. Lecture theatre. MICHAEL is back in front of the class.

MICHAEL: So all of this… *(MICHAEL indicates the complicated mess of squiggles on the board.)* is just my fancy shmancy way of saying something that another great mathematician once said. Anyone heard of Bing Crosby? For every complex idea in the universe there is a song lyric that sums it up beautifully. I've just spent two hours explaining the ins and outs of subjective probability when I could have just sung you a song about it.

MICHAEL sings a few lines of a maths-related Bing Crosby song to his students, ending on a big flourish.

ALISON appears at the door. She stands there while all the students exit past her. She walks over to MICHAEL, nearly banging into a student.

ALISON: *(Shouting after them.)* Oi! What's the fucking hurry? *(Under her breath.)* The vending machine's not going anywhere you fat – *(To MICHAEL.)* Well I nelly-never. Look who's back with a-fucking-vengeance.

MICHAEL: That's my favourite lesson.

ALISON: Lesson? I thought I was in Vegas. *(Beat.)* It's good to have you back, Michael. I didn't know you were in here. I only came through to chalk your board up.

MICHAEL: To what?

ALISON: Force of habit. I chalk your board up so the Dean thinks you're here. You're the only one who ever uses chalk. No need for that, now.

She tosses the chalk over her shoulder.

ALISON: Welcome back, Michael.

She hugs him.

BRIAN appears. ALISON immediately and unsubtly exits.

MICHAEL: Shouldn't you be at Fairy Towers?

BRIAN: I didn't go. I didn't want to. It... It was the other guy I liked.

MICHAEL: So you liked the geeky guy with the big brain but you ended up with the cute guy with the big willy?

BRIAN: I like you. Can we go for a drink?

MICHAEL: I'm afraid not. I've got work to do.

MICHAEL goes over to the blackboard and draws two rectangles on the board.

BRIAN: You don't need to be worried about me being your student. I –

MICHAEL: I'm not worried. Why would I be worried? I'm leaving.

BRIAN: How come?

MICHAEL: Once I've done the maths part of my study into my deluge of attraction theory and made the formula for my genetic model for homosexuality with testable predications, I'm leaving.

BRIAN: No way. *(Points at the board.)* Is that it?

MICHAEL: It is. That's Fairy Towers. It's my complex system. I just need the data.

BRIAN: Where will you get the data?

MICHAEL: The field data? I'll get it from the field.

BRIAN: But you would basically need to get into every single one of those flats to collect the data. *(Pause.)* You're not going to sleep your way through your complex system?

MICHAEL: Adam has to.

BRIAN: He doesn't *have* to. *(Pause.)* Come for a drink with me. A hair of the dog.

MICHAEL: I can't. I'm doing this.

MICHAEL turns his back on BRIAN and starts scribbling on the board. BRIAN stands and stares at him for a bit and then exits. MICHAEL covers every inch of the board with equations and diagrams. When he has finished he goes to the lectern, picks up his briefcase and heads for the exit but when he gets to the door he turns and comes back in. He takes a bottle of wine from his briefcase and he pours himself a glass.

6.

It's later and BRIAN is dancing in a nightclub across town. 'Relax' by MIKA/'It's In Your Eyes' by Kylie/'Human' by The Killers/Something upbeat but melancholy.

At the same time JOHN is in Daphne's Bar clearing the tables and shutting up and occasionally dancing to the music in the bar.

MICHAEL is still in the lecture theatre. It is covered in crumpled pieces of paper. He has written equations on all the boards, on notebooks, on sheets of paper and on the OHP. Dishevelled, drunk and exhausted , MICHAEL is still scribbling.

MICHAEL's students come into the lecture theatre.. He stands in front of the lectern holding a single sheet of paper.

MICHAEL: Okay, so right, so basically, what I'm talking about is a genetic model for homoseggsuality…homoseggs – gayness, generating testable predixons… Tasteable depictions – safe bets. So my idea was – well actually, to give him his due it was this guy John I shagged the other night's idea – You see you have two tower blocks, right? Let us calls these FT. Now suppose you've got a fairy, small f, per flat, big F – You have at least one, sometimes two, three or more – dirty bastards. Now you can only imagine what goes on in these towers. Actually let's call them S and G – Sodom and Gomorrah. Or sodomy and gonorrhea, which is more bloody likely. And you've got me. I'm the ex. I'm the stalking, psychotic ex. I'm the constant. Now my theory was that if I have sex with everyone in both the towers – And before you get all shocked and Open University on me, it doesn't have to be full sex. It could be a little blowy or a ham shandy. That's fine. So where are we with our testable de-pic…our safe bets? Well… hundreds of research hours, three bottles of wine, over seventy imaginary shags later… After the chucking away of years of PhD, I have to admit it, I have an un-workable system, and what do I do with one of those? *(Beat.)* Don't be scared, I can take it. I throw it away.

MICHAEL screws the piece of paper up and tosses it away.

MICHAEL: Mind you there was one bit that looked vaguely promising.

MICHAEL gets down on the floor and searches through the piles of paper.

MICHAEL: Where is it? Where are you, you little shit? Where's my e equals m c squared gone to?

ALISON rushes in and takes the papers out of MICHAEL's hands. She darts around gathering up the papers. She looks up at the students. She stares at them.

Pause.

ALISON: Get out of here you…you voyeurs! *(Pause.)* Get out!

The students start leaving the lecture theatre. ALISON gathers all the papers off the floor as they leave. MICHAEL collapses against the lectern. Once all the papers have been cleared, ALISON wipes the whiteboard. Finally she dusts the blackboard. She goes to MICHAEL, puts her arm around him and guides him out the theatre.

7.

A week later. ALISON is in the lecture theatre in front of a class of students.

ALISON: I am a scientist. And, okay, I admit it, I'm a cynical bitch. There I've said it. I'm a torn-faced, scathing, cynical scientist who thrives on putting people down, even when they don't deserve it. Even when women who could find gainful employment in a circus, lifting caravans with their bare hands, *aren't* banging into me in the corridor or knocking me over in the canteen as they respond to irrepressible rises in their blood sugar. Scientists are often guilty of forgetting about that which lies outside science. Like love. Like the presence or absence of love. Now, I'm not saying that what I've been doing over the past few days with a…new person in my life is love. In fact as an activity it probably falls somewhere between wrestling and gymnastics with a bit of Pilates thrown in. But whatever's happening to me, and long and hard may it continue, it's made me realise that there are some things that fly in the face of mathematics, logic and theories, because love isn't just something that you do, love is true. And wherever Michael has disappeared to – And incidentally, as you can imagine he's burnt his bridges with the Dean – her extraordinary patience has run out – and he won't be back. I hope he realises that he's missed something out from his equation and I hope he finds it. I hope he finds love.

ALISON packs her stuff up and picks up MICHAEL's briefcase as the students leave. All except BRIAN who walks over to her.

BRIAN: That was lovely.

ALISON: I can act gay too, Brian, I just know when to rein it in.

BRIAN: It's great that you've met someone.

ALISON: Met someone? I've practically swallowed her. The Dean and I are like a pair of boa constrictors. *(Beat.)* Michael's not been at his flat for days. He'll be on a bender somewhere, won't he?

BRIAN: I don't know. Are you worried about him?

ALISON: I don't think he's topped himself, Brian, if that's what you mean.

BRIAN: Well, I fucking hope not.

ALISON: You're actually quite endearing for this completely and unsolicited-ly omnipresent person, Brian, but can't you see Michael is just not that into you?

BRIAN: You're right. *(Beat.)* You are a bitch. You're a torn-faced, cynical –

ALISON: Fuck off.

BRIAN: I'm in love with Michael. *(Beat.)* I'm hardly going to make his life worse at the moment, am I?

Beat.

ALISON: Maybe you should look for him.

BRIAN exits.

8.

Later that evening. Daphne's Bar. The bar is completely empty. BRIAN walks in. He has rolled-up posters in his hand. He goes up to the bar. He waits.

BRIAN: Hello?

He looks around.

BRIAN: John?

BRIAN unrolls a poster. It has 'missing' written across and a picture of MICHAEL. He puts it up. JOHN appears, wearing sunbed goggles.

BRIAN: Hi, John. *(Pause.)* It's me…Brian.

JOHN: I know who you are. *(Removing his goggles.)* They've just delivered my sunbed. I've been lying on a UV beach with a cocktail. Why not, eh? There's bugger all customers in here.

BRIAN: Is it OK if I put this up?

JOHN: What is it? What kind of club night is 'Missing'? Is there a dress code? I was at an underwear only club, last night. They should have called it Underwear Only As

Long As It's *Not* From Primark. I've never seen so much boil in the bag.

BRIAN: It's not a club night. It's Michael. He's missing.

JOHN: Then get it down. We don't do missing posters here. I'm trying to run a pub – encouraging people to enjoy themselves, not showing them pictures of the recently departed.

BRIAN: He's not dead.

JOHN: How long's he been missing for?

BRIAN: A week.

JOHN: Maybe not then. I suppose he is quite cute. You can leave it up, but only if you buy a drink. Where have you been looking?

BRIAN: This is the first place. I've just started.

JOHN: What? Well, he's not missing then. He's just out on the town. He's having a good time somewhere. And you need to find out where he is. Hire a detective. There's ones that specialise in boyfriends.

BRIAN: He's not my boyfriend.

JOHN: Whatever. I'm not one to judge. Your daddy, your master, your fuck buddy…whatever he is. Do you know his Gaydar password?

BRIAN: No.

JOHN: What am I paying my taxes for? I thought you were supposed to be intelligent.

JOHN goes over to the leaflet rack and picks up a map of the gay village.

JOHN: Right. So he's in a square mile most probably. Now we could just go and run round every venue but I'm not a chicken anymore and you're not exactly light on your feet.

He's not into techno, is he? He doesn't look like he is. Does he like cheese?

BRIAN: I don't think so.

JOHN: There's a science fiction themed bar. Would he go there?

BRIAN: No.

JOHN: Good. We'd have to call off the search if he was in there, wouldn't we? What does he like?

BRIAN: Um. Um. He likes…

JOHN: You don't even know what he likes? Is there's any point looking for this guy?

BRIAN: He likes maths. He likes Bing Crosby. He likes singing Bing Crosby songs. He likes singing maths related Bing songs. Where could he do that?

JOHN: I don't know. Try the old folk's homes. *(Beat.)* Oh my God have you tried the Hollywood Show Bar? I swear to god he's at Karaoke happy hour on the top floor of the show bar, sandwiched in between a couple of trannies. They sing shit like Bing Crosby in there. Hang on while I shut this dump.

BRIAN: Are you coming?

JOHN: Of course, I'm coming. It's kara-fuckin'-oke.

JOHN and BRIAN exit.

9.

The top floor of the Hollywood Show Bar. MICHAEL staggers in the corner. The backing track to his Bing Crosby song starts and MICHAEL picks up the microphone and starts singing. JOHN and BRIAN enter but MICHAEL doesn't notice them. JOHN picks up a karaoke songbook and quickly leafs through the pages. BRIAN cautiously approaches MICHAEL. MICHAEL doesn't stop singing. Eventually, MICHAEL clocks BRIAN, drops the microphone and stumbles towards him. JOHN urgently fills in a karaoke slip and hands it in.

MICHAEL: I've had a couple of drinks already, Brian. I'm a little bit…fucked. I forgot you were coming.

BRIAN: I wasn't.

MICHAEL: No? What you doing here then? Like a bit of karaoke? You just missed my Bing. It was great. I had everyone up.

BRIAN: I saw you.

MICHAEL: Did you? What did you think?

BRIAN: I loved it.

MICHAEL: Shut up?

BRIAN: I did. I loved it. It was the best thing ever.

The karaoke backing track for 'Islands in the Stream' *by Dolly Parton and Kenny Rogers starts playing. JOHN picks up the microphone and rushes it over to BRIAN.*

BRIAN: What's this?

JOHN: You know what this is. Sing!

JOHN backs away. BRIAN stares at the video screen, the microphone down by his side.

JOHN: Sing.

BRIAN sings a couple of verses of the song to MICHAEL.

JOHN grabs the microphone off BRIAN. MICHAEL throws his arms around BRIAN. They stay in this embrace, swaying, BRIAN occasionally supporting MICHAEL.

JOHN takes over singing the song in the background. The song goes into instrumental.

MICHAEL: What are you doing here?

BRIAN: Looking for you.

MICHAEL: You found me. Tah-dah! How did you know I'd be in here?

BRIAN: By taking all the possible venues in the gay village and calculating the various club nights and events on throughout all the venues. Setting parameters of taste, clientele and drink promotions and then tabulating all the possible bedrooms, hotel rooms, parks etc... John worked it out.

MICHAEL: John?

BRIAN: *(Pointing at JOHN.)* Him. He used a hybrid system of intuition, private detective work, common sense and subjective probability.

MICHAEL: Everyone's a gay pseudo-scientist these days.

BRIAN: Everyone is capable of thinking. Even without diagrams, Michael. Evolution doesn't have a rule book.

MICHAEL holds BRIAN closer.

MICHAEL: Okay. Okay. Not so loud. *(Beat.)* This is nice.

BRIAN: The singing?

MICHAEL: No. This. You. *(Beat.)* If only I wasn't your lecturer.

BRIAN: About that... You know when you were crawling around the floor of the lecture theatre searching for the obscene equation you'd made up prior to disappearing of the face of the earth?

MICHAEL: Vaguely.

BRIAN: Doesn't that worry you at all, you know, professionally?

MICHAEL: It's academia. A certain level of eccentricity is encouraged.

BRIAN: I'm afraid you've gone the graphic illustration of a knob hanging off the balcony of a block of flats beyond that.

MICHAEL: Oh, right. Well. Yes. I guess I burnt my bridges then.

BRIAN: You could say.

MICHAEL stands back from BRIAN, takes his hands and stares into his eyes.

MICHAEL: How did I manage to resist you?

BRIAN: Well, you know, when a man wants to find a genetic model for homosexuality generating testable predictions, other things tend to get sidelined.

MICHAEL: I'm a fool.

BRIAN: You're my fool.

They kiss.

While JOHN sings the final chorus, BRIAN guides MICHAEL out of the bar. JOHN doesn't notice. He stays and finishes the song before rushing out.

10.

A few days later. The lecture theatre. MICHAEL, all sorted out, stands at the lectern.

MICHAEL: So, to draw all this nonsense to a conclusion… Although we could be forgiven for thinking that by logical reasoning and rigorous deduction we can find an answer to everything. And the vast number of different applications of mathematics suggests to us that we could put the world to rights with a calculator and a piece of paper – of course we can't. And although we feel powerful, almost omnipotent when we make observations about the patterns of things around us – whether that be single cells or great groups of things, matter…people… The known universe is a tiny spec of focussed understanding in the midst of an endless galaxy of mystery. Why am I telling you this? Why am I gushing? Well…I guess I don't want you to find yourself on a park bench telling complete strangers that Pythagoras is speaking to you through the shapes around you. *(Beat.)* And I guess I feel like telling you that just because you can do things with maths, just because your science gives you a bit of power, you have to decide yourselves how to use it. Oh, and love. Love doesn't obey any laws. Love doesn't add up. Love cannot be tracked down and hunted using subjective probability, trigonometry or origami. You can't cheat love. The answers are always at the back. The end is always at the end. Subjective probability is about patience and integrity and should never be used in a desperate attempt to get your lying, cheating ex-boyfriend back. You should love maths with every set of compasses, set square, ruler, and graphic calculator in your pencil case. I know you all do. That's why you're still here. But more importantly and I'm speaking to myself as much as to you, you should love love. What's the point of being at university without having a little bit of love anyway? Even Alison's making her bed squeak at the moment, with the Dean, of all people. D'you think they smile at each other? Of course they do. Listen, feel free to leave at any time, I'm just gushing. This isn't part of the course, you can have this for free. I'd like to thank you for having me back. And thanks to whoever it was who dropped the indecent exposure charges.

MICHAEL packs his stuff up. BRIAN rushes over to the lectern and hugs MICHAEL. ALISON enters.

ALISON: Very touching, you cheeky bastard. Glad you didn't feel the need to come back apologetically.

BRIAN: He doesn't need to apologise. He's got a mental health problem.

ALISON: And a spokesperson, too, I see. *(Beat.)* I'm proud of you, Michael. It's great to have you back. And it's great about Adam, I mean Brian, it's good to get something back from the students. Aren't you tempted to spend his student loan and then chuck him?

MICHAEL: What's up with you? Does the room not match your outfit?

ALISON: Why do you say that? What's wrong with my outfit?

BRIAN: You look amazing. You always look amazing.

ALISON looks away and blots away a tear.

ALISON: *(Turning back.)* It's just, Michael… I'd like to drop this cold exterior and…and give you a hug for a moment but –

MICHAEL goes over to ALISON and hugs her. She grips him back tightly.

ALISON: Okay. That's enough. I'm done. Thanks. See you later.

ALISON scarpers.

MICHAEL: I love her. She's my favourite mathematician.

BRIAN: Are you sure you're ready for this?

MICHAEL: Why, are you getting cold feet?

BRIAN: I don't mean us. I mean maths. You mustn't rush into it.

MICHAEL: I feel fine. I feel great. I feel better than I have done for years.

BRIAN: If you ever feel like you did before, you have to tell me.

MICHAEL: I've got something to tell you. Yesterday, I got an email.

MICHAEL takes a folded piece of paper out his jacket pocket.

MICHAEL: I was going to delete it.

BRIAN: But you printed it instead?

MICHAEL: I was going to burn it.

BRIAN grabs it.

BRIAN: *(Reads.)* Dear Michael. I attach a pdf file with derivations of an equilibrium frequency of a 'gay allele in a model of sexually antagonistic selection which assumes that the allele is located on the X-chromosome.' What the fuck?

MICHAEL: It's from Professor Gavrilets. He's a leading bio-mathematician in the US. I sent him an email when I was doing the study. Apparently there's something in it.

MICHAEL grabs the piece of paper from BRIAN and rips it up. BRIAN kisses MICHAEL and exits.

11.

Later the same night. In Daphne's Bar. The bar is busy. JOHN is dressed to kill, mic in hand, standing on the top of the bar. He starts a karaoke backing track to a high energy pop song and sings the first verse.

BRIAN and MICHAEL enter. They have to squeeze into the bar and find somewhere to stand. JOHN waves to them as they enter.

JOHN: *(Speaking over the track.)* Where do you go my lovely? Where do you go? It's a question we've all had to ask from time to time and it's a question that I hope we'll find the answer to at our Where Did You Go My Lovely Lost Boyfriends Karaoke Night. Now how did that dozy old queen come up with an idea like karaoke missing persons, I hear you cry. Well if you spent less time guzzling horse tranquilisers and more time in the company of mathematicians from the University of Manchester you might find you have the odd thought yourself. Now, tonight is all about finding boyfriends that have disappeared into the scene. It's already worked for our very own Brian and Michael. That's that chicken that just came in with his dad just now. Now, have I got this right, Michael, you had a nervous breakdown after failing to discover a genetic model for homosexuality generating testable predictions? Michael tried to get his boyfriend back in the usual way we do, by spending about a hundred grand's worth of university research money on developing a complicated equation to prove to Adam that their relationship was the result of millions of years of evolution. But it didn't work, did it? Not so fucking clever now. And he ended up in the Hollywood Show Bar. Well it's happened to all of us, hasn't it? You'd not go in there if you were right in the head in the first place, would you? And then Brian traipsed in here, one night a few weeks back, and I thought, hello, I was just going to have a pizza for dinner, but it looks like I'm having chicken instead. Anyway, Brian was looking for Michael and I helped him find him and if you want to know how and to discover my unique patented mathematical system for finding your lost soul mate… You'll have to buy a drink and I'll tell you.

(Sings.) Where do you go
My lovely?
Where do you go?
I want to know
My lovely.
I want to know.

JOHN gets down off the bar and presses through the crowd to where BRIAN and MICHAEL are. They group hug.

BRIAN: This is great.

JOHN: Isn't it? It'll pay the electricity bill. That sunbed's cost me more than a fortnight in Fuerteventura. You two look great. Are you making lots of tasty dinners for each other or something?

BRIAN: We're just happy. Aren't we?

MICHAEL: Yeah, really happy.

JOHN: *(To MICHAEL.)* And are you alright?

MICHAEL: Yeah.

JOHN: I mean really alright? Sometimes folk tell you they're fine and then you find out they're building a crucifix on their balcony.

MICHAEL: I'm fine. I'm back to my old self.

JOHN: Well you're not going to get back to your young self.

BRIAN: I'm looking after him.

JOHN: Of course you are, darling. Students are excellent at looking after people. Grub on a grant – yummy. Right. *(Taking their hands.)* Come on. Let's make some fucking money.

JOHN drags BRIAN and MICHAEL through the crowd and the three of them climb up on the bar and share JOHN's mic. They sing the final chorus of the song together, building to a huge finale.

The End.

UP

Up was first performed on Monday, 10 August 2009 at The Vault, Edinburgh for the Edinburgh Fringe.

CAST

ROBERT, Laurie Brown

CREW

Director, Rosalind Sydney
Sound Designer, Danny Krass

A hospital bedroom and en-suite toilet. Early afternoon.

The curtains are shut. The lights are out. The bedroom door opens and sounds from the corridor drift into the room. ROBERT slips in and shuts the door.

ROBERT: We were right about the custard. There's something going on there... I don't know what exactly. Don't worry – I ate it all. There was loads of it but I made no fuss, I ate it all, it seemed to work.

He sits on his bed.

I've reached the point in the story where I do as I'm told. It's hard to believe I functioned on my own before I had their help with everything. Maybe I didn't – maybe I just believed I did. *(Beat.)* When it finally happens, that's it, end of story. You don't have to do anything any more. No one's help is required. It's almost too good to be true. It's suddenly even easier than eating custard. *(Pause.)* You left at the wrong time. We had a laugh after you went.

Steven was sick. He hates being sick, you can tell, poor little fucker.

It was Paul. He thinks it's clever. *(Beat.)* Paul doesn't know what I'm thinking. I don't fucking care if he does, but he doesn't. Nobody knows what's going on in my head. I'm not thinking what you might think.

There's nothing wrong with secrets. Who tells other people everything? Sometimes it's only a story to you. If you told other people they'd be like 'that's not a story. Fuck off.' I know that. I haven't told anyone this story because... This story began in the Eighties and it's still going on to this day. It's mine. It's like my fucking life story. In the film of my life... *(Pause.)* You'd cut most of it.

He walks over to the mirror and looks at himself.

I fucking hate custard. I would never choose to eat it but I ate it today. It doesn't make sense does it? I hate Paul. I've probably only known him a few weeks but I hate him with a passion and it's not a secret it's just a fact that I haven't shared with anyone until now.

He studies himself in the mirror.

I'm a naturally skinny person. There's no arse in these trousers. You see, I don't eat custard as a rule of thumb.

ROBERT sits back down on his bed.

You skipped pudding today, Stuart. Why's that? Not hungry? Neither am I. I'm eating for two – boredom and agitation. I could still eat. I could eat a packet of crisps.

He picks up a litre bottle of Coke and gulps much of the contents.

Though the story may change, the ending remains the same. I have locked the door and I hold the key. There's a slight lack of suspense in that set-up, which is probably why I am eating so much. I'm comfort-eating my way out of my own boring story. I've failed at this before. I could never get the horror out my head and put it down. So I locked it away. I locked thousands and thousands of my words away. I did what they told me to do and put them all in a drawer. And then I became a teacher.

If I'd been any good... Any good as a teacher... If I was still teaching and I had a class, and in my class I had teenage boys... And someone Paul's age, with all that aggression, with that bare chest, strutted into the room with his hand down his trackies gripping his dick... I'd say, 'I'm sorry, I'm not teaching that.' *(Beat.)* Dave says Paul doesn't mean anything by it – he says it to other people. He doesn't mean any of it. *(Pause.)* Have you heard him saying to anyone else that he wants to... *(Beat.)* After you went to your bed he came over to me, got right in my face... So close I could see beyond the yellow teeth and scarred skin and... He's not bad looking close up, I thought. I don't know why I thought that, I was terrified of him too. He knew what I was thinking. He saw me search his face. 'Out my fucking body, cunt! Out my fucking body, ghost cunt, or I'll stab you in the cock with my fork.'

Imagine what you could do to a cock with a blunt fork.
Look what he's done to our heads. Imagine the damage.
Imagine the damage you could do with a pen never
mind a piece of cutlery. You could stab someone with a
pen, Stuart. You could Bic someone to death. I couldn't
personally, I don't think. I would have to go insane first,
properly mad, I'd have to go fucking mental… None of
the nurses took any notice. Not even Dave. I must deserve
it. What am I, a paed' or something? No. I'm fucking not.
(Pause.) Paul reckons we're in here for something more
than just sickness but it's his sickness that makes him think
that. He thinks I'm a paed', Stuart, so I'm treated like one.
He thinks I'm a ghost too, he really fucking thinks that.
You're a silent witness because you never say anything…
But what does that actually mean? Fuck all. It's like a child
would make up. Dave's the fat policeman because he tells
Paul what to do but it's his fucking job, isn't it. What's
Paul? What the fuck is Paul? Is he really what they say he
is? Who does he think he is? Probably thinks he's Jesus.
He's some kind of nasty Jesus who would stab folk in the
cock with a fork.

If he came at me with his fucking fork he'd be on the floor
in an instant with a nurse on top of him and a syringe in
his arse. *(Pause.)* That's not a turn on for me by the way.
I'm feeling relieved, that's why it makes me feel…happy.
I'm feeling…I'm not turned on. I'm not turned on by that
little bastard.

*Suddenly there's a loud bang on the wall of the corridor followed by
a cackle of laughter.*

(He shouts at the door.) Leave me the fuck alone, you twisted
little cunt. What the fuck's wrong with you? You're not ill,
you're evil. You're just some evil little bastard aren't you?
Some evil, stepdad-murdering, bastard.

*ROBERT starts to hyperventilate. As he does he retches. He tumbles
into the en-suite toilet, and throws up violently in the sink.*

Jesus Christ, look at that stuff. Thought it would never stop coming. I could have drowned. It's good I'm not lying on my back like I'm meant to be. I'd be choking. I'd be inhaling stomach acid into my lungs. You'd have to put your fingers in my mouth, Stuart. Get them right to the back of my gullet and claw out chunks of chicken pie, pureed potatoes, broth bits, cakey pineapple. If I was unconscious, you'd have had to put your mouth, to my slimy, sick-covered lips and blow through a film of hardened custard. You'd have to. Not that I'd fucking want you to, Stuart. I'm thinking about me dying here and you saving my life… I don't have a fucking hard-on here for fuck's sake. *(Pause.)* That's not a skinny man's lunch, that's obscene. I got that in a hospital? There's three litres there. That's an overdose. *(Pause.)* I'm glad I got that out of my system. Thanks, Paul.

How can I think this shit and have the audacity to appear again and again, day after day? If I lurched across the room, Stuart, ripped down your trousers and gobbled your cock what would I be then? And what am I now for thinking about it?

You get to a certain point and think you couldn't do it because you don't have the strength but the strength doesn't come from us, in fact, it's not strength, it's momentum. It was easy putting the cable in my mouth the other day and turning the little red switch from naught to one. As the power surged in, I thought – gosh, how simple was that? Almost accidental – I thought – it's dangerous that, I better warn other people about it. Getting jolted across the room took more effort, but none on my part. It threw me across the room like a piece of rubbish, like a fucking piece of shit. *(Pause.)* It's never as easy as you might think.

ROBERT crawls back to his bed.

In act five, scene three, Juliet stabs herself in the chest with a small dagger and we imagine that with a single puncture wound she died. Probably not though, probably she was still at it half an hour of forty-five minutes later, desperately trying to make a deep enough cut. In fact, if Romeo had arrived a tiny bit earlier he might have found her thrashing about in a pool of blood and had to humanely assist her passing. I've always thought of myself to be more a bottle of vodka and a packet of pills kind of guy until now. I'm weak. I'm in a kind of comfort zone. That's why I'm still here. I shout at doors not faces. I don't have it in me. I turn pale and I throw up.

ROBERT peers over at STUART.

Are you listening, Stuart, or are you sleeping? *(Pause.)* Come for a fag with me. Paul's out there in the corridor. He'll smash my head in if I'm on my own. But I think he's scared of Silent Stuart. I'm sure he reckons you're a witch. Will you come with me? I'll leave you twos.

Pause.

I'm absolutely not to smoke in the room again, Dave says, so… *(Beat.)* Absolutely not – it's so emphatically negative, that. It's so soppy-stern. It's so camp and British – almost flirtatious. I'm sure I said it. Havoc going on all around me in the classroom and I pipe up with 'Absolutely not acceptable.' Might as well have blushed and called them naughty boys. Paul, you murdering little bastard, you are absolutely not to stab any of the other boys or myself in the cock with a fork, you naughty boy.

A long pause.

Those boys were obsessed with gay, Stuart. *(Pause.)* It was as though gay had got into their heads somehow and was ricocheting around. All it took was this slightly weak looking, long streak of nonsense of a man… They knew what I was in instant. I'd better keep this down or the cock-stabber might hear.

(Directly to the audience.) At the start it was words. One word in fact. One single word I could easily have said – that I wanted to say – that if I'd said... It was his fault. He started it. He flicked his thick, shiny fringe out of his eyes, smiled broadly, showing off those dimples and said, 'Do you want to suck my cock, Sir?' *(Pause.)* 'Yes.' That's all that would need to slip out. 'Yes.' That would be enough to ruin everything. 'Yes.' I was kept awake at night, terrified by the short hiss of the word. It quickly gathered momentum from there. If it was easy to say yes, how only slightly harder it would be to take it further. 'Do you want to suck my cock, Sir?' 'No, I want to fuck your arse.' A little bit of anger could make it all so easy. I bit my tongue, literally, through all his lessons. I bit it hard. The pain was a deterrent but I was convinced it would happen one day. 'I want to lick your bum and fuck it,' I might say. Imagine that. I imagined it. All the time. I couldn't get it out of my head. I rehearsed what I would say to the head teacher, you know, once it had happened. He was disgusted but he kind of understood. It was my fault, I shouldn't have done it but I was in a stressful situation. Or maybe I wouldn't get to speak to the head teacher. Maybe a policeman would stand with me while I cleared my desk. All for saying yes. All because it's an easy little word that hisses out your mouth without you thinking about it. The fear of what might inappropriately trip off my tongue spread. It seemed such a plausible fear. Worse that my terror of impulsively grabbing an arse in the corridor. Imagine that. You'd be beaten by an angry mob and rightly so. You can't walk around grabbing arses just because you have mental health problems. You can't be a teacher and grab arses. I got past that anyway. I got to grips with it. But in every exchange there is the opportunity to blurt out an insult. It's terrifying. But, I never have. I never did it. I never said anything out of turn to anyone out there. Not even the nasty boy with the nice eyes. I didn't say anything to him.

ROBERT goes to the bed and puts his headphones on.

RELAXATION TAPE: Just like riding a bike or driving a car, we can learn to relax. You can use this systematic relaxation programme in all situations.

ROBERT: I told Dr Elyot that thoughts are a punishment. He said 'what for?' I said, 'Thinking.' *(Pause.)* I don't think he got it.

RELAXATION TAPE: Absolutely not to be used whilst driving or operating machinery.

ROBERT: That young nurse is looking through the door again. What age must he be? Nineteen? It's like one of my students has turned up to see what they've done to me. You didn't do this to me. This didn't happen in the classroom.

RELAXATION TAPE: You should make use of this recording somewhere you feel comfortable, somewhere that you can really relax.

ROBERT: Like when you're locked in Ward 4 being threatened by a teenager who has murdered before?

RELAXATION TAPE: You can relax in all situations. Find somewhere you can be really comfortable, like a bed or an armchair. Make yourself as comfortable as you can. If you do need to respond to anything, like the telephone or a knock at the door, you will of course be able to do so.

ROBERT: Will I be able to respond to the overwhelming need –

RELAXATION TAPE: Yes, you can wake up and become fully alert at any point in this unique systematic relaxation programme. Begin by closing your eyes.

ROBERT: I wish it was that easy, love. I'd shut my eyes, roll over and sleep if I could, but it's not going to happen.

RELAXATION TAPE: Don't resist it.

ROBERT: I wouldn't be resisting anything, I would be forcing them shut. You said all situations. My situation is that this is my last relaxation tape.

RELAXATION TAPE: Let your jaw relax. As your jaw relaxes so do all the other muscles of your face. Let your face relax.

ROBERT: Very soon my face will be totally and utterly relaxed. My family will come and see me… I won't be able to hurt them from beyond the grave. I won't be able to slam the lid of my coffin on their heads… 'At least he's peaceful now,' Mum will say, 'He looks like he did before all of this started…'

RELAXATION TAPE: As you relax your face let your mind relax. Let your face be calm and your mind be still.

ROBERT: God gave us a perfectly good method for relaxing.

RELAXATION TAPE: Relax.

ROBERT: You can't do it here without someone coming to frustrate your efforts. How they distinguish between that and the sound of me scratching my arse…

RELAXATION TAPE: Your legs and arms become heavy and they melt into the bed like thick heavy oil.

ROBERT: If only…

RELAXATION TAPE: Relax the large muscles of the gluteus maximus.

ROBERT: I have, believe me.

RELAXATION TAPE: Now let your mind relax.

ROBERT: Can't we linger longer on the arse?

RELAXATION TAPE: Forget your body and let your mind relax.

ROBERT takes a deep breath and releases it slowly.

ROBERT: I'll have a fag and then I'll do it.

RELAXATION TAPE: You don't need to do anything. Do what you choose. Tell yourself what you want to do.

ROBERT: I want to do it. This is it. I'm at the point in the story when it happens.

RELAXATION TAPE: Tell yourself you're going to be happy.

ROBERT: No.

RELAXATION TAPE: More fulfilled, more creative.

ROBERT: My story began in the Eighties.

RELAXATION TAPE: You'll laugh at it all one day.

ROBERT: I already have.

RELAXATION TAPE: These potent messages go deep into your subconscious.

ROBERT: Good.

RELAXATION TAPE: Nothing has happened.

ROBERT: It has. In Lomond Ward – I thought I'd escaped…

RELAXATION TAPE: Nothing has happened. We are at the start. We're at the beginning.

ROBERT: I thought I'd escaped from places I could jump – from things I could take, stairs to trip down, poisons to drink…

RELAXATION TAPE: In the beginning there was nothing.

ROBERT: There was no danger. There was no Paul, no Paul's fork, there was just mealtimes, medication and mile after mile of farmland. It seemed OK.

(Directly to the audience.) I taught myself to think about the possibilities. I have always seen the potential dangers of objects, thoughts and desires. For a long time I associated these thoughts only with ice-skating – A combination of the cold air, fizzy drinks and 'I Think We're Alone Now'. The first time I put on a pair of ice skates, when I was a kid, I felt like I had two large razor blades on my feet. What if I didn't swerve just then and skated over that man's hand and chopped those fingers off? What if I fell on the ice, as I so often did, and I let my legs thrash freely, slashing the limbs of those who crashed into the back of me? Later on,

in Dad's car on the way back to Mum's I agonised about it. Why had I thought that and what did it mean? 'Couldn't those blades do a lot of damage, Dad?' I asked anxiously 'Oh yes, Son, you could split someone in two.'

I can't sleep, I've tried the tape, I'm having a fag.

ROBERT goes to the smoking room.

ROBERT: I slept during the day yesterday so I was up all night smoking. I tried to stay in bed for a bit but I started checking, Stuart. I was checking my response to you, Stuart, to your breathing. Your breathing was… I felt like it was irritating me. It wasn't all that bad but…but then I became aware of the pillow in my hands. I had to get away from it. I was scared I might do something with the pillow to stop the breathing. I went to the smoking room. I stayed there for hours smoking, listening to your breathing from down the corridor and resisting the urge to run towards it. I smoked all my fags. At about half five I was holding my last one. I'd been holding it for an hour, delaying the inevitable end to it all and…Karen was in and out of the room every half an hour with a face like a suicide note. I made her talk. She didn't want to fucking talk in the middle of the night, it was doing her head in. I was passive smoking her fags as well. I was active/passive smoking her fags, Stu…versatile smoking them, you could say. When she breathed out, I breathed in. Dave came in and lit it. I was leaning against the wall, about to nod off. He said 'smoke your fag and then go to your bed, Robert.' My bowels were telling me to stub it and run but I kept going. I stood up, padding from foot to foot and sucking on the hot, crackling fag. When I reached the writing I stubbed it and bolted to the toilet. I'd hardly sat on the seat when I exploded. Nicotine in water dribbled down the china. The aftershock was ripping at my lower abdomen. I took a deep breath and came though here.

ROBERT comes back into the room.

I looked out the window and saw the crack of dawn, the smallest crack. It gave me the energy to tumble onto my bed. The fear of my pillow subsided, it won't be back until tonight. That's how you were spared, Stuart.

ROBERT goes over to his bed, rummages around underneath it and takes out a wrap of newspaper. There is a knock at the door. ROBERT freezes. A piece of paper has been shoved under the door. He goes to the door and cautiously retrieves it. He takes it to his bed and opens it.

(Reading it.) Respond to the following statements with emphasis on the way you would describe yourself before you used the systematic relaxation programme. One. I felt anxious. Give your anxiety a numerical rating, one to ten.

He writes as he speaks his answer.

(Writing.) Just before doing the systematic relaxation programme I caught a glimpse of a young man staring through my door and it reminded me that earlier in the day I had basked in the simple beauty of his face. I rate my anxiety as zero. I must add that his face was like relaxation foreplay to me as I had been at anxiety level ten or thereabouts for most of the day.

That should smoke him out if he's interested. If he offers to help me shave next time, we'll know why, Stuart.

(Reading.) Two. I felt agitated. Give your agitation a numerical rating, one to ten.

(Writes.) Six.

I'm saying six, Stuart. That should get me something, eh? If I say ten they'll think it's bullshit. I'll get something for six.

(Reads.) Three. Death is imminent. Give this a numerical rating, one to ten.

(Writes.) Before doing the tape I felt like I was about to die. I was at ten. I was at ten yesterday as well. I've been at ten all week. I've been at ten for weeks and months and years.

Which is quite stupid when you consider the fact that I'm still here. Well, I am going to die. Today. I am going to die before you come and take me to the TV room. Ten.

'Four. I felt unsafe. Give this feeling a numerical rating, one to ten.'

(Writes.) As a feeling I would rate this feeling as a one. Feeling unsafe is a shitty, shitty feeling. Personally I would feel safer if I was on top of a hill in a dark house, receiving disturbing phone calls, than I do just being me, here, now.

ROBERT goes over to the door and shoves the paper back under it. He stares through the window down the corridor.

My secondary school was just one long fucking corridor, Stuart. It was one long fucking corridor with rooms leading off it. The school I taught at… For those few weeks. I say taught, I simply stood in a room filled with young people, holding my tongue. I was only there a few weeks. I was on supply. That's all. That school revolved around an enormous courtyard. Everything radiated out from it. It was a great statement about… Something… Positive. At my own school they didn't want us hanging about so all we had was a corridor with rooms of the same size, leading off it. How inspiring. Like a blank advent calendar – plain white with un-numbered doors. Why open any of them? The outside world was just another one of the rooms off the corridor. I used to forget which it was. I would open a door, expecting fresh air and get a lung-full of chemistry instead, or jeers from the gym hall… *(Pause.)* I believe that there's a door in here that opens onto that corridor. *(Pause.)* I open the door to the long corridor, dressed as I am, holding these, *(He holds up the pencils.)* and walk in. It's between periods. I can't see any friends. I better just stand with my back to the wall. I'm given a wide berth at first. It's a shock. I look shocking. I would in a corridor, in a school. I cause a clot in the corridor as people stand around staring, pretending not to look, but staring at me out the corners of their eyes. I almost fitted in, in the classroom, in a suit, not so long ago, now I'm being bumped into by boys who have realised what I am. I'm a fucking ghost. I'm an apparition from the local mental hospital. I'm stood in the corridor of my own school. I'm the most unsuccessful former pupil ever to return. They grab the pencils from my hand. 'You're welcome to them,' I scream 'Take them off my hands.' 'You're doing me a favour.'

ROBERT holds up the pencils in front of him. He lines his thumbs up with the nibs.

The pencils lurch back towards me and freeze in front of my face.

ROBERT presses his thumbs against the nibs, snapping them.

They snap them before my eyes. I don't appreciate that. I don't have anything to hold onto now. I can't remember where the door is to the outside world or I would run for it. I come back in here. I shut the door behind me.

ROBERT shuts the door behind him.

I found these in my bed yesterday lunchtime.

ROBERT walks over to his bed holding the pencils up in front of him.

Thinking is a punishment for thinking it.

He sits on the bed.

Where the fuck did they come from? Are they yours, Stuart? Did you put them in my bed? Where did you get them? Can you even write? I'm not taking the piss. Can you write? It's just that you don't seem to be able to fucking speak to me or to anyone else. You can't write, can you? Please tell me. Tell me if it was you that hid these fucking pencils in my bed. Speak to me.

ROBERT takes out the pencils and studies them.

They haven't been written with. They're brand new, Stuart. They must have been a present from someone. Did someone bring you them and you didn't know what to do so you hid them on my side of the room? It's OK, if you did. I don't mind. It's a little bit thoughtless but… Maybe they're the last person's. *(Beat.)* Why were they in my bed though? *(Beat.)* Did the cleaners find them and put them there? Why would they? Do you think they might play tricks on us? Maybe they do. *(Pause.)* Maybe someone brought them. A gift. A pair of fucking pencils – what kind of a present is that? What kind of treat is a couple of sharp pencils for your mad pal in hospital? 'I just couldn't think what to take him so I took him a couple of pencils…'

ROBERT lies on the floor next to STUART's bed.

How do you keep it so together, in here, with me? I draw out every tiny aspect of my life in front of you and I haven't even got to the point. Well now I'm at the point when I get to the point because there is a point. There was a point and there is a point. The point was, Stuart…

I fancied him. Fin. Fin with the fringe. Of course I did. We all did, but I was too old… I had undisclosed feelings. That's why the words were so impatient to appear on my lips. I wanted him. Yes, I wanted him. I wanted to suck him. Damn fucking right. I wanted to lick his arse. I licked it, in my mind every night. I still do sometimes. I lick his seventeen-year-old arse. And if you could get away with a wee wank in this place without someone pressing their face against the door I would be licking his arse and shooting my load right now.

ROBERT plays with STUART's shoes, lying by the bed.

How long have you been in here? Longer than me? Longer than Paul? I bet they wouldn't stop Paul. I'd like to see them try. How come you're not climbing the wall? Is that your meds? Don't you fancy it? Fancy it raw? Why not? *(Pause.)* I need you, Stu. I need you to take my mind off… Take my mind. Take me. I need you, Stu. I need you to explode inside me. It might reach my brain and in a last vain, glorious attempt get this stupid shit out of my head. Fuck this fucking shit out of me head, Stuart.

ROBERT puts the shoes back and sits in the centre of the room staring up at the window in the door.

It's not all about me. I know that. It's… My ego joins the dots up with a chunky wax crayon. Or felt-tipped pen gripped by four fingers like the hand of a child and it makes connections. And those connections put me at the heart of the story. A story that began – say – in the Eighties, and it's still going on to this day, telling itself to whoever will listen. But it's not *his* story, it's *my* story and it's not about them. It's not about anything. It isn't about God or the Bible or Jesus. It's just a load of joined-up dots that were never meant to be joined, they just have been. But try telling that to your inner-screaming-fucking-baby. All he wants to do is join the fucking dots up. So the reason you're here isn't because of some, like, great misfortune and it isn't just another event in your life that could pass by unnoticed. It's for some great plot of…something else, and if you search the corners of your mind you might discover it, like I did.

(Directly to the audience.) This story began in the Eighties, at secondary school, in third year, just before my prelims. It was modern studies. I hated it, I hadn't done any revision. All I could remember was a photo of Gorbachev kissing a man and something about proportional representation. My stomach was tied in a knot. Why wouldn't it be? It didn't know it was going to be multiple choice, a piece of piss, fucking easy. We were all in the same predicament. My friend Martin had been listening to his personal stereo in every lesson through a single headphone he'd run down his sleeve and stuck in his ear behind his cupped hand. It looked like he was just leaning on his hand and concentrating when really he was like listening to Nirvana and writing 'life sucks the big one' over and over on the inside of his folder. He was shitting himself. That's when he told me about the boy with the pencils. The boy from another school. The urban legend. He was being deliberately vague. I knew that. I didn't know he meant

me, though, in the future. I was the boy with the pencils. I was then, am now and will always be the boy... The boy was nervous. He hadn't revised for his finals. He was sat in the exam hall with a pencil case, a blank piece of paper and an empty head, except for this one thought that had been ricocheting around for some time, about pencils...

ROBERT holds his two pencils up.

From his pencil case he took out two pencils. They were sharp. It was the only thing he had done to prepare for the exam – sharpening those pencils.

ROBERT studies the pencils.

Whose two HBs are these? What the fuck were they doing in my bed, Stuart?

I came here wearing smart clothes, Stuart. Do you remember? Paul called me the suit, remember, the burned-out business man? Fucking genius, eh? I was on supply. I was on my way back to school, Stuart. They needed an English teacher at short notice. I was all that was available. It wasn't until I tried to sober up for the eight o'clock start on the Monday that I realised just how mashed my head was. I tried to relax over the weekend. I tried to calm down the wine and the fucking cigarettes. I wouldn't be able to leave the classroom every fifteen minutes for a fag for fuck's sake. On that Monday morning – just a few weeks back... That's it. That's all, eh? Fuck.

ROBERT goes to his bed and brings his crumpled suit out from under it.

On that morning I put my suit on and stood in front of the mirror and I said aloud, 'who the fuck are you trying to kid?' I looked at myself properly for the first time in weeks. I didn't look human, Stuart. There were dark circles under my eyes. My arms were heavy, my shoulders were stiff...uncomfortable. I looked like a cunt. Maybe I just need another human to react to. Perhaps the kids will force me back to being myself. Maybe you'll get Fin the fringe. Don't say that. What if I say yes? *(Beat.)* Don't take yourself so seriously, it's a fucking job, just do it. I put my coat on, drained a cup of coffee and stuffed some paracetamol...

He rummages in the pocket of the suit trousers frantically and then stops abruptly.

And this fucking thing, Stuart. I found it comforting. The feel of the cold metal. I was planning to play with it in my pocket while I stood in front of the class. It was going to take my mind off smoking.

He takes out a metal pencil sharpener. The kind with two different sized holes.

What's the big hole for on these? It would make a really short nib, wouldn't it, Stu? What's the point? It must be for something we don't do anymore, something we never did when I was at school either.

ROBERT carefully sharpens both of the pencils and watches himself in the mirror as he does.

The invigilator doesn't notice – she's not supposed to be watching them yet. Everyone else is staring at her – the large woman from another school in the suit at the front of the hall, or at the enormous clock that isn't normally there, loudly counting them in to examination hell. And no one notices the boy inhaling pencils. *(Beat.)* My story began in the Eighties. In a corridor. I'm still in a room off that corridor. My story began in the Eighties and it's a story... that has to end. I want the story to end. I want it to come to an end now.

When I saw myself in the mirror the day I was planning to return to work I could have pissed myself laughing. If I'd been someone else I would have. I would have pissed my suit trousers at me – Look at me. What a cunt. Good fucking luck with that one.

ROBERT goes through the bathroom and inserts the pencils into his nose.

The exam paper lay in front of him. He never opened it. He swung back on his seat for the last time and then threw his head and pencils on his desk.

ROBERT throws his head onto the sink. He cries out in pain. He does it a second time. He gargles and chokes and yelps in agony.

Long pause.

Are fifteen year olds' noses different to ours, Stuart? Are they softer? I was so worried about doing this, I didn't bother to question whether it would work or not. *(Beat.)* And it didn't, did it? *(Beat.)* It never fucking worked. End of story.

Blackout.

The End.

ACKNOWLEDGEMENTS

Julian Forrester, Polly Clark and all at Cove Park, David MacLennan and all at A Play, A Pie and A Pint, Julie Ellen and all at Playwrights' Studio, Scotland, Steven Thomson and all at Glasgay!, Ros Philips, Drew Taylor, Sergey Gavrilets, Nicola McCartney, David Leddy, Zinnie Harris, Linda McLean, Kate Temple, Laurie Brown, Danny Krass, Mark Kydd, Jonny, Mum and my heroes Ros Sydney and Kram.

WWW.OBERONBOOKS.COM

 Follow us on www.twitter.com/@oberonbooks
& www.facebook.com/oberonbook